HEART STRINGS

SARAH'S STORY

MAGGIE LYNCH

Windtree
Press

Windtree Press
Hillsboro, Oregon
http://windtreepress.com

Cover Design by Christy Carlyle, Gilded Hearts Design

Heart Strings / Maggie Lynch. -- 2nd ed.

PRINT ISBN 978-1-947983-49-6

EBOOK ISBN 978-19400641-6-1

❀ Created with Vellum

This is for Terri Reed, a wonderful author with more than twenty books with Harlequin Love Inspired and Harlequin Suspense Inspired. She has always shared her knowledge, her faith, and her heart with other writers. Through reading her books and getting to know her, she taught me that writing a story with characters who consistently live their faith can provide the best example of living a spirit-filled life.

This is also for Jessa Slade. Thank you for the writing retreats, the ear for discussing character arcs, and for your great analysis of story. Thank you for helping me stay on track and to keep plugging away even when times are hard. You are beautiful and smart, a combination that many would envy. As for me, I simply feel blessed that you are in my life.

Dear Readers,

It is finally time for Sarah's story. If you've been following Sarah's role in the band through the first two books, you know she is the quiet one. She is different from the other band members in that she takes her faith very seriously, and sometimes it puts her at odds with people in the band who don't understand or agree with her thinking. Some believe she has led a sheltered life. Nothing could be farther from the truth.

Sarah has been steadfast in her belief that sex only happens after marriage. This has been a source of teasing from some of her band mates, and sometimes a source of embarrassment for Sarah. Pummeled by the realities of modern dating practices, it has also been a tenet that she questions for herself.

In today's world it is rare to find someone who sticks to that rule —particularly someone well into her twenties. However, I have personally known a number of young women who believed strongly that they wanted to save themselves for their husband and stuck to that belief no matter what. I've known other women who were widowed or divorced who also decided not to have sex while dating, instead waiting for remarriage. The decision is highly personal and not for me to judge. But, within the confines of a romance, it is key in how I present Sarah's story

As you learn about Sarah's background, her faith, and the struggles she has in living her life, I hope you will root for her to find her truth and live it with confidence. For Sarah, faith is easy…but living is hard.

CHAPTER 1

TOM PAWLAK AWOKE WITH A JERK. Eyes wide, he peered through the shadows above his bed. Sunlight cast a bright haze through the barn slats. Unwilling to get up, he closed his eyes and rolled away from the light, scrunching the pillow beneath his head.

"Dammit!" He tossed the pillow aside and raised himself to sit on the edge of the bed. Thoughts of Sarah had kept him up all night. Why did Jack have to bring her up last night? He'd been here two years caring for the old man and not once had he mentioned his daughter. But last night, in a drunken stupor, Jack wouldn't shut up about her. The one woman Tom had ever loved. The one woman he should have married.

The one woman who would never speak to him again.

He heard barking outside the door. He reached for his jeans and T-shirt and pulled them on quickly. The jeans were too loose these days. He grabbed his belt and pushed it through the worn loops, tightening it to the last hole. He'd lost about twenty pounds over the last few months. Working Jack's farm along with a job in town had taken a toll on him. He needed a new pair of jeans. Ones that fit. But he didn't even have time to shop.

The barking grew louder, more frantic. Then a man's scream.

Tom rushed outside to find Kip, the border collie, running in circles and barking his head off. Billows of smoke poured out the front windows of the farmhouse.

Jack! He stripped off his shirt and doused it with water. Holding the T-shirt to his nose he threw open the screen door and scanned the living room. No flames. He pushed through the smoke, toward the kitchen. His heart slammed in his chest.

Flames had already climbed the curtains above the sink and were licking along the ceiling. The all-wood structure would go up quickly if he didn't act.

"Jack!" He called as loud as he could between coughing spats. "Jack!" He listened for any sound of a voice.

Fire now engulfed the end wall and baseboards, immediately claiming cardboard boxes, newspaper and other flammable material along the way. Horrified, Tom pressed a hand to his mouth. In the smoky haze, he sprang toward the sink and turned the cold water on full force. The dog's barking now joined with two other dogs outside.

Tom took the sprayer and pointed it at the flames. The water stream barely reached most of it. He had to get the garden hose. But where was Jack?

Wheezing, Tom rushed outside, located the hose and, with quick twists of his hand, cranked it on full blast. He jerked it free of the wheel and ran back into the house, uncoiling the entire length of hose behind him. He doused the living room and then made his way back to the kitchen, spraying until everything in sight was completely soaked. Then he went searching for Jack.

"Jack," he called again, moving through the house and checking each room.

In the back bedroom a dresser had fallen over. He quickly pulled the dresser upright. Jack lay unmoving on the floor.

"Jack? Are you all right?" He kneeled next to him and pressed his hands against his neck checking for a pulse. It was strong. How did this happen? Why was Jack back here and the fire in the kitchen? For that matter why was he even out of bed?

Jack's eyes fluttered open. He looked confused.

"What happened?" Tom asked.

"I needed a drink."

"At six in the morning?"

"I don't care what damn time it is. I needed a drink. I have a right to a drink don't I? Don't give me any back talk. I'm dying. I can have whatever I want."

Tom chuckled with relief. Obviously Jack wasn't hurt. "You've always had whatever you wanted, Jack. If you want to kill yourself, I'm not gonna to stop you. But you're not taking me with you." He squatted behind Jack, wrapped his arms around his chest. Then with one long pull, he lifted him to a standing position. "Can you stand on your own?" He slowly released his hold.

Jack took an uneasy step forward then turned. "I'm fine. Damn dresser never was reliable."

"What happened?" Tom scooted the dresser back against the wall. "How did the fire start?"

"I was lookin' for my whisky. As I reached for it, my fat belly hit the stove and it turned on a burner. The flame caught my shirt. I took off my shirt and threw it on the stove. I turned off the burner, but by then my shirt was goin' like gangbusters and it caught the curtain. So I grabbed the whiskey, came back here, closed the door, and prepared to die."

Tom's fists clenched. Yes, Jack was dying and it sure didn't make him any nicer.

"Did you consider that by the time the fire got to you the whole house would be gone?" he asked, his breath barely escaping between clenched teeth. "Did you consider the barn would have burned and I would have died too?"

Jack closed his eyes.

"Look at me, dammit!"

Jack opened his eyes and stared past Tom.

"It's one thing you deciding to kill yourself. You made that decision when you kept drinking." Tom pointed his finger at Jack. "But don't make that decision for me. I'm not ready to die."

Jack sighed long and loud. "Dammit, Tom. I can't even die properly. What the hell am I supposed to do?"

"You're going to take it like a man," Tom snapped. "It's not pretty and it's only going to get worse, but I refuse to let you hurry it along by giving up or killing everyone else around you."

Tom shook his head. It had been a bad night all around, and the morning wasn't shaping up to be any better. He'd have to spend most of this week fixing the kitchen and living room. And that would take money--money neither of them had, but there was no way he would let Jack die in complete squalor with no one he knew nearby.

"I still don't get how the dresser fell on you." Tom scanned the room and noticed clothes were strewn from the door to the window. "Were you looking for something?"

"Yeah." Jack yanked open the bottom drawer and the dresser teetered.

Tom quickly righted it. "I'll have to nail the backboard to the wall so it won't tip again."

"I wanted that damn document Lizzie left me. The one that says this house belongs to Sarah. Figured if I was gonna die, at least Sarah could see she got the house."

"A burned-down house, Jack. What good would that be? You could've asked me, you know. I would've gotten it for you."

"Sure you would, but you wouldn't get me my drink. I can't stand that look you give me every time I wanna drink. Like I'm the devil or something."

Jack held back a long sigh. Long ago he'd decided not to try to stop Jack from drinking. But every time he handed a bottle to Jack he knew he was helping him die faster.

Resigned, Tom said, "You're not the devil, Jack. But it's drinking that got you to this point. Would it really hurt to wait till afternoon to have a drink?"

"I'm dying, dammit. I'm not going to change my ways now. I'm no hypocrite; I'm an alcoholic. So what? There's no way in hell I'm goin' to heaven; so I might as well go out enjoying my whisky." Jack sat on the edge of the bed and poured himself a glass of whiskey from the large bottle on the nightstand. Then he crawled back in bed and took a long drink. "Now leave me to my vices. You're livin' here free, go make yourself useful. If I'm awake around noon I'll join you for lunch. Now get out."

Tom shook his head as he turned and walked toward the door. He wasn't exactly sure why he'd volunteered to help care for Jack. It's not like Jack had asked for help; and he definitely never voiced any appreciation. Tom closed the door solidly behind him and headed back to the kitchen to start the clean up and repairs.

As he eyed the slurry of ash and paper on the counters and the floor, Tom couldn't help laughing at himself. Karma was biting him on the ass. No doubt about it. This was definitely payback for Sarah. All that talk last night, Jack's request to get Sarah back here before he died, and Tom's subsequent dreams were telling him something. Something he didn't really want to face.

He knew why he stayed on and cared for Jack. Jack helped him and his mom when they needed it most. When his mother was in the final stages of ALS, two years ago, Jack had taken pity on them. He'd come around a lot and actually helped take care of his mom when Tom had work in town.

And when she'd died, it was Jack who'd help pay for the funeral; and it was Jack who went with Tom to spread her ashes along the Mountain Fork River. When the landlord came and kicked Tom out of the shack he'd grown up in, Jack offered him a place in the barn in exchange for help around the farm.

Two years since his mom died. Two years he'd been living in that barn for free. Yup, Tom owed Jack. The least he could do was make him comfortable in his final months. The doctors said his liver was poisoning him and it wouldn't be long before it got the job done.

Jack wanted to see Sarah one last time and Tom had promised he would get her out here. Problem was no one knew where Sarah was now. The last address Jack had was three years old and evidently she didn't live there anymore.

All Jack knew was that she lived in Oregon and played guitar in a band named something Canyon. And he wasn't even sure of that.

Tom did know one thing for sure: she'd hate seeing him again. Though Jack had forgiven him, he doubted Sarah ever could.

CHAPTER 2

SARAH PUT DOWN HER PEN and scanned the chords she'd written. She turned sidewise from the kitchen counter, re-tuned her guitar, then plucked the chord changes once more. Something wasn't right. The G to E minor chord worked well in the beginning section, but the transition to the chorus section didn't resolve right. She tried C to E minor, and then C to G to D. It sounded good, but not right. She scratched the chords above the lyric and hummed it the way she had envisioned it.

> *I close my eyes to draw you near.*
> *Teach me, Lord, to simply hear.*
> *Lead me through the muddy dark.*
> *Help me mend this broken heart.*

B7! That was it. First D, then B7 as it rose, then back to E minor to resolve it. She scratched out the previous sequence and wrote in the new changes. This was her first original song with Sweetwater Canyon and she wanted it to be perfect.

A burst of the swinging door nearly slammed into Sarah's back.

"Oops. Sorry. Didn't see you there." Kat opened the fridge and stared at the interior. "It's got to be close to lunch time, don't you think?"

"It's always meal time for you. Where are the others? Have Rachel and Michele arrived?"

Kat pulled out a carton of orange juice and some type of onion dip. She made a big deal of closing the refrigerator and then pouring a bunch of pretzels into a bowl on the counter.

"I'm not *always* hungry, just most of the time. I can't help it. I'm a teenager. We're supposed to eat."

"That looks real tasty," Sarah said, though she couldn't help wrinkling her nose. How did orange juice and pretzels go together? She loved Kat and her mother, Theresa. But she'd never understand teenagers eating habits. She was sure that when she was a teenager she ate better than this.

When Sarah left Broken Bow, Oklahoma and arrived in Oregon seven years ago, Sweetwater Canyon was just forming as a band. It was Theresa who saw Sarah playing at a local farmers market and invited her to join them. At that time, they had Rachel on fiddle and a bass player named Kelly. Kat had always been on accordion and Theresa played guitar, mandolin, and banjo. When Sarah showed up, Theresa was really happy to find another guitar player so she didn't have to play hers as much.

Sweetwater Canyon was more than a band of musicians. It was her family. She'd left Oklahoma not really knowing where she wanted to end up. She'd packed everything she owned and headed west until she'd driven out the pain from home. She knew nothing about Portland, but she'd trusted that God would lead her to a better situation. And He had. Sweetwater Canyon became a family that stuck together even in really tough times, and never gave up or abandoned each other.

Though she and Rachel hadn't immediately hit it off, Sarah had grown to love her like an older sister. They still disagreed on lots of things, but they respected each other. When Michele took over for Kelly, Sarah felt that she was the sister she never had. And Theresa and Kat were the kindest souls she'd ever met.

Sarah smiled and stood. Yes, she was very blessed.

Kat cocked her head to one side. "Something good?"

Sarah rounded the kitchen peninsula and gave Kat a hug. "Yeah, I love it here. I'm just happy you're part of my life—you, your mother and the whole band." She grabbed a pretzel and took a bite. "I even love you and your crazy orange juice and pretzel snacking."

"You okay?" Kat asked. "I mean I know I'm cute and all, but this huggie stuff all of a sudden has me worried."

Sarah waved the song sheet at her. "I'm finished. My first original song and all is right with the world."

"Cool. We going to try it today?"

"That's the idea." She couldn't help grinning. Finally, she felt she could really contribute to the band. She'd been with them for seven years and had never had the confidence to write her own music. It had taken her that long to put the past behind her. Now that she'd finished this one, she knew there were more inside waiting to get out.

"Hey, where's the baby?" Rachel said from somewhere outside the kitchen.

"He's not a baby anymore," Michele answered as the two of them came through the door. "He's four now and in pre-school. In fact, he's really excited about kindergarten next year."

Theresa came in last. "Orange juice at 7pm, Kat?"

"I was hungry." Kat pointed to the pretzels and dip. "I'll share."

Theresa rolled her eyes. "It's a wonder you are still so thin. You just had dinner an hour ago."

"Really? Was it that long ago?" Kat opened the pantry. "I better get something else to take to the rehearsal then. I'll be starving after the first song."

Everyone talked at once, checking in with each other, catching up with the news, making plans. Sarah smiled. Yes, this was definitely her family.

Sarah's phone vibrated in her pocket. She turned her back and gingerly held it up to see the number. Her father. She shook with disbelief. When was the last time he called? Two years? Three? They weren't exactly on the best of speaking terms. She took a deep breath and let it out.

"Excuse me," she said into the cacophony of voices. "I need to take this." She left the kitchen and retreated to a quiet corner of the living room and accepted the call.

"Hello." She tried not to let the fear in her voice be heard.

A moment of silence made her wonder if she'd misread the number. It wasn't that she didn't want to speak with her father. It was that she didn't know what to say.

"Hello? Is this Sarah Cosgrave?"A male voice. Unfamiliar. Definitely not her father.

"Yes, may I help you?"

"Sarah?" She heard a deep breath, as if whatever was coming would be difficult. "This is Tom. Tom Pawlak."

The name sucked the moisture from her mouth, stilling any reply from her tongue. Sarah's chest constricted. She couldn't breathe. She sank into a chair before her legs betrayed her.

"I know it's been a long time." Tom said. "Are you sitting down?"

It was just a phone call. Why was he calling on her father's phone?

She cleared her throat. "Yes, I remember you Tom." She felt that sounded official, as if it didn't matter. Of course it mattered. He was the one and only man she had ever trusted. He was the one and only man she'd ever let close to her. The one who betrayed her trust in men … forever.

"I'll just get to it then. I'm sorry to deliver this over the phone. I've been trying to locate you for the past three months. I'm afraid that your father is dying. I don't know how much longer he has. The doctors say three months, I think it's shorter. He wants you to come, Sarah. I suggest you make it soon."

Her racing heart skipped a beat, like the wheels of a bicycle hanging in the air as it hit a large bump then crashed to the ground. She waited for the numbness to dissipate and the weight of the usual pain to wash over her. But it didn't come.

She should feel something. Something other than this cold void. What was wrong with her? Maybe she needed time to process. She guessed she owed it to him; but she wasn't sure she wanted to be there at all. Her father had never been there for her.

When she'd left Broken Bow, she swore she'd never return. She swore she'd never put herself in a position to be hurt again—by her father or Tom Pawlak.

"Sarah?"

She looked up to the ceiling and counted the wooden beams that spanned the breadth of the living room. Those beams held up this house—Theresa and Kat's house. The house she now considered her real home. A home built on a foundation of love and trust.

How was it that the two men who betrayed her were now bound together in this way? Why was Tom Pawlack the one to call her? What had happened in her absence?

Sarah vacillated. She really didn't want to go. She really didn't want to face her past. She'd run away for good reason and found a home with Sweetwater Canyon. Did she have to leave the one safe place she loved?

She closed her eyes in resignation. "Thank you for notifying me, Tom. I appreciate you taking the time to locate me. However, this is not a good time for me to go to Broken Bow."

"Wait, Sarah, I—I'm—afraid there's more. Something about your mother."

"What about my mother?" She struggled to keep her voice from shaking. Her mother died when she was just a little girl, eight years old. Her father had always had whisky around. But it was her mother's death that gave him the excuse to drink from sun up until he finally crashed for the night. And she was left to fend for herself. To try to run the farm. There were neighbors who helped for the first year, but then they gave up too. They didn't see that helping did any good.

"It's the house." Tom let out a big breath. "The house belonged to your mother, Sarah, not your father. It was always yours. Your father would have given you the deed after you graduated high school...if you hadn't run away."

Sarah waited in the uneasy silence. She didn't care about the house. She'd left all that behind. A tear traced down her cheek. Why was she crying? She didn't care about anyone in Broken Bow anymore. She owed her father nothing. She owed Tom nothing.

She knew what her faith said. Honor your father. Even if he never loved her. Why did it have to be so hard to follow that commandment?

"Please, Sarah. Please come home. He needs you. That's all I can say."

"But I don't need *him*!" she shouted into the phone.

"You know you have no choice," Tom said, his tone coaxing. "I know you. You won't turn away from this."

The dam burst and Sarah shook with the bottled up anger she'd never been able to shove back at him. The unkept promises. The betrayal. Breaking her heart.

She paced the room, each step revving her anger higher until she was stomping. "You do *not* know me, Tom Pawlak. You never did and you never will. Don't tell me I have no choice. I'm not under my father's thumb or yours anymore. I don't have to come. What did he ever do for me except drink, carouse, and pretend to mourn my mother's death? I don't owe him anything. And you, of all people, have no right to judge me."

A long silence made her wonder if Tom had hung up during her tirade.

"I accept that." Tom said, in a whisper. "I deserve that. But it's been seven years. You have every right to hate me, but not your father. There were good times before your mother's death. I remember you talking about them. You can at least honor those memories with him."

She couldn't speak. She clutched the phone so hard that her entire arm ached.

"He's dying," Tom continued, his voice urgent. "Whatever he's done, you need to say goodbye. If you don't, you'll regret it for the rest of your life."

She couldn't rustle up any compassion but she knew Tom was right. Though the lack of love her father showed her after her mother's death still stung, he did not deserve to die alone. She would follow the commandment to honor her father. She would care for him and pray for him in his last hours. And she would do everything possible to avoid Tom Pawlak.

There was no commandment about honoring ex-jerk-boyfriends.

She gathered her courage to speak. "Thank you for your call, Tom." She stood and straightened her spine and made sure her voice sounded definitive and assertive. "Please, let my father know I'll be there in two days."

"Thank you." Tom's voice sounded tired. "Let me know your itinerary and I'll pick you up at the airport."

"I'll make my own arrangements. I can take care of myself." There was absolutely no way she was going to spend two hours with him on the drive from the airport to the farm. "I'll take the shuttle."

"Sarah ..." She listened to the long pause before he spoke again. "I know I deserve your scorn, but we have to work together to make your father's last days the best possible. What happened between you and me was a mistake, and I take full responsibility. But it was also a long time ago. I was young and scared and stupid. Please let me help you now. Let me pick you up from the airport. I can tell you all the circumstances around your father's care on the trip back to your father's house."

"What circumstances? I already know about the drinking. I lived it. Remember? I always knew it would kill him."

"It's best that I tell you everything after you arrived."

"No. Tell me now."

Silence.

"What are you afraid to tell me? What's worse than him dying? There is nothing you can tell me about his life that is any worse than I already know."

Silence.

"Tom?"

"I'm the one who is caring for your father. I'm living here with him now."

Sarah sucked in a breath. How could this be? Tom was not a responsible person. He couldn't be trusted. What had he done to weasel his way into her father's life in his last days? When Sarah had left home, even her father said he'd shoot Tom Pawlak if he ever stepped on his property again.

"Sarah?"

"Give me a minute. I'm trying to take it all in." She swallowed hard. "I ... don't understand. What do you mean, exactly, when you say 'taking care of him'? If he's dying, why isn't hospice there? Or a home nurse or something?"

"He didn't want strangers in his house. He wanted someone who would understand him, his choices. I've been taking care of the farm. I'm also his caregiver."

Dread walked up her spine and circled her chest, squeezing so hard she was certain her heart would stop beating.

"How long?"

"I've lived here for two years," he said again. "I've been his care-giver for one year."

How did she not know? When was the last time she'd spoken with her father? She searched her memory. When was the last time she'd called? Or written a letter? Dear Lord, the last recollection she had was sending her annual Christmas letter two years ago. Or was it three? She hadn't sent one last year because Sweetwater Canyon did so many holiday gigs that time got away from her. The year before, she couldn't really remember what she was doing around Christmas time two years ago. Her father never wrote or sent a card. She was always the one reaching out. How did she let so much time go by?

"If you are living in the house, where am I to stay? There are only two bedrooms."

"I'm not in your bedroom," he said in a voice she could barely hear. "I built a small room in one side of the barn. Things have changed a bit since you were last here."

Sarah's mind kept circling around her past life, one that she now feared could destroy whatever happiness she had made in Oregon. She pulled into a hunch and clenched the phone even harder.

"I have to go now, Tom." Her voice strained to get sounds out. "I'll let you know when I have plans made." She debated whether or not to ask for his email. She really didn't want him to have hers. Then she realized how petty that sounded. After all, she would be seeing him face-to-face very soon. "Please send me your email address. I'm at SarahC19@gmail."

"Thank you, Sarah." His gravelly voice sounded as if he'd been talking for hours. "I'm sorry to be the bearer of bad news. I'm truly glad you're coming home. I'll see you soon."

She heard the click as he disconnected the phone. She stared into nothingness. She welcomed the numbness now. The void enclosed her, keeping the fear out. She finally felt something. And it was awful.

MICHELE SAT on the sofa clasping Sarah's hand. Theresa was on her other side, fussing with a cup of tea and exhorting her to drink. Rachel and Kat sat opposite the sofa in the two club chairs.

"I'll take care of the tickets," Michele offered. "I'm good at finding flights."

"And don't you worry about us," Theresa said, patting her hand. "We'll be just fine, and we can talk on the phone every week if you want."

"Or even every day," Kat said. "If I were in your shoes I would want to call home every day."

Sarah managed a wry smile. "Thank you, Kat. I might need to call more often."

"We can take turns, so you can always have the phone on and be with one of us. Maybe not when you're asleep, I guess you don't want that. Or in the bathroom. That would be a big yuck."

Sarah held up her hand. "I don't need 24/7. But thanks for the thought, Kat."

"So, this guy who was such a jerk to you" Rachel said. "Is he at least good looking?"

Leave it to Rachel to go directly to the lets-look-for-the-sex possibilities. Though, since the court trial and her marriage, she'd calmed down a bit.

"Yes, he's the jerk. As for what he looks like, I don't know," Sarah said. "I haven't seen him in seven years."

"What about seven years ago, then?" Kat pushed.

"I guess," Sarah said. "I mean he wasn't exactly ugly."

"At least you have that, then." Kat twisted a strand of hair around one finger. "I mean I know you hate him, but maybe he has changed. Maybe…you know…you two can get back together or something."

"That is *not* going to happen." Sarah smiled to take the sting out of her angry retort. At seventeen, Kat still believed in fairy-tale love. Though she'd experienced betrayal herself, she still maintained a trust in men and relationships that Sarah didn't understand.

Sarah turned to Theresa. "I really don't know how long I'll be gone. The doctors said three months, but Tom believes things will move quickly. If you need to get another guitarist, I completely understand. I know that spring is the time we always start touring."

Theresa patted Sarah's hand again. "We are *not* going to get another guitarist. If a gig comes up and you're still gone, I'll pick up your guitar part. You just take as long as you need. When you're ready to come back, we'll be here waiting for you. There is *always* a place for you in the band."

Sarah's eyes moistened. When God brought Theresa to her, it was the best gift in the world. While she was with her father, and facing demons from the past, she would cling to the promise of coming home to her Sweetwater Canyon family.

CHAPTER 3

HANDFUL OF TINY SNOWFLAKES splatted on the front windshield of Tom's truck as he made his way to Will Rodgers Airport in Oklahoma City. Soon the flakes turned to rain and the clouds darkened. Even the weather had conspired to punish him for his past.

The one hundred and ten mile drive each way would be brutal—not for the driving, but for the anticipation of Sarah's arrival and the dread of her anger for the entire two-hour drive back to Broken Bow. What in the world did he think he was doing? He'd been fine on the phone talking to her. It didn't take as much courage to ask her to come to her dying father's side when he didn't have to look her in the eyes. But actually facing her … what was he thinking?

When he'd started taking care of Jack, he'd never imagined Sarah coming back. In fact, Jack had never mentioned her until the other night. Tom had imagined her married with a couple of kids by now. It wasn't until Jack mentioned he wanted to see her and that he hoped she and Tom would get back together that he realized she was still available.

Chances were good she would welcome neither him nor his apology with anything resembling open arms. And if he were being honest, he knew that Sarah wasn't the only one who would not be in line to welcome him back in her life. Likely the whole darned town would do everything in their power to make sure Sarah didn't make that mistake again. Between Jack's drinking and Tom's reputation of carousing, angel Sarah would be encircled and sheltered by the entire community. The church ladies would take it upon themselves to protect her from both of them.

He'd done all of them wrong, more girls than he cared to count and their families, including the pastor's daughter. That was his rebellion against a God that would treat his mother so poorly and let her die in such an awful way.

But it was the rich girls he'd sought most. Back then he thought every time he seduced a rich girl he was shaking his fist at the town's elite. He was proving to them he was more than they thought … better than his economic circumstances suggested. But it turned out the rich girls had the last laugh after all.

After he and Amanda had run off together, he learned she was using him as much as he was using her. She called it slumming. Getting it on with a bad boy was a rite of passage among some of her friends. After their one weekend together, Amanda made it a point to give his phone number to all her girlfriends. It got around town that slumming with Tom Pawlak was the best way to get back at your parents. Doing it with the poorest guy in town and letting your parents know was the fast way to the in crowd and all the hot parties.

When there were no girls left wanting to rebel, he ran away. Just like Sarah. For four years he wandered from town to town picking up farm jobs, missing Sarah, and hating himself for what he'd done to her. He tried to settle down, get in some college, figure out who he was meant to be. Then his mother got sick.

When he came back to care for his mother, he'd tried to make amends with the town. Most of the rich folks had moved on to greener pastures, so it wasn't as hard as he expected. However, he still couldn't bring himself to go to the church where Sarah had grown up and where his mother was a member.

The downpour increased and he flipped his wipers into double time. The precipitation wasn't enough to start flooding streets yet; but it was a big annoyance. With a sigh and a shake of his head, he braked to slow and pay better attention to the road.

The two-hour drive would give him plenty of time to figure out a way to beg forgiveness for his behavior with Amanda … and all the other girls of Broken Bow. He didn't deserve a second chance, and he wasn't asking for one, but he was man enough to admit that Sarah deserved an apology. Even this many years later. She'd been nothing but kind, loyal, and loving, and he'd treated her poorly.

He'd tuck tail and grovel if he had to, not only apologizing to Sarah, but doing his best to make it up to her before her father died and both of them moved on with their lives. He only hoped she didn't run him off Jack's property before he'd had a chance to prove that he was no longer that scared kid who'd betrayed her trust, her love. No one would ever again love Tom the way Sarah had and he lived with that every day.

TOM WATCHED Sarah place her guitar case next to her as she watched the luggage carousel spew out bags. He couldn't get over the changes in her. She'd always been good looking in an innocent-girl-next-door sort of way. Her oval face, long straight blonde hair and full lips had always attracted him. That and her faith that no matter his upbringing, he could make something of himself.

The cute girl he remembered now had feminine curves encased in perfectly fitted stonewashed jeans and a white collared shirt belted to show off her waist. She rooted in her purse and pulled out a rubberband. Her long fingers quickly divided her caramel honey-blonde, waist-length hair into three sections and braided the entire length of it.

He had a strong urge to take his time and undo that braid in the privacy of his bedroom and see finally hold her in his arms. He shook his head. No way was that going to happen. He would not take the chance of breaking her heart again. Or his.

A large man muscled in front of her to snatch his suitcase from the carousel. Sarah patiently waited for him to move, then repositioned herself closer to the carousel so it wouldn't happen again.

He watched her bite a cuticle and then worry her lower lip. He swallowed hard. Perhaps some innocence still remained.

Shame rolled through him at the things he'd done seven years ago. It didn't matter that he truly believed she was too good for him and knew, if he hurt her, he would never have to face her hurting him later. It didn't matter what the excuse, he shouldn't have let hatred of himself spill over on her.

When Sarah drove out of town, he thought she'd be back. He thought he'd have time to figure out a way to make it up to her. He didn't know how much he'd miss her. Yup, he succeeded real well in not just breaking her heart, but locking up his own and throwing away the key.

SARAH FINALLY SPOTTED they red strap wrapped around the worn grey suitcase. She widened her stance, one foot in front of the other, ready to wrestle it off the carousel. Grunting as she tugged it toward the rail, she jogged alongside it not letting it go as she tugged harder. With one last pull she maneuvered it off the carousel and rolled it back to where her guitar remained.

She'd had difficulty packing. Not knowing how long she'd be staying or what types of chores she might need to do, she was pretty sure she'd managed to squash an entire closet into this one large suitcase. Most of it was jeans and a variety of shirts to go with them. Jeans had been her daily wear when she'd worked the farm in Broken Bow, and it had remained her outfit of choice for band gigs, shopping, or just hanging out around the house—that is when she wasn't in PJs or sweats for the day, trying to match music to a lyric.

She'd packed three dresses for church, and gone out of her way not to pack anything for a date night. The last thing she wanted was to give Tom, or any guy in town, any sign she was available. She wasn't.

In fact, outside of church and the occasional grocery store run, Sarah planned to stay at the farm. She would make sure she and Tom rarely crossed paths. All she had to do was to get through this two-hour trip from the airport and she'd be golden.

"I'll help you with that," Tom's voice said from behind her.

Sarah's stomach dropped to her knees. With tons of dread—and more curiosity than was healthy—she took a deep breath and steadied her nerves. She turned to find Tom holding a tan cowboy hat with one hand against the heart side of his chest.

He placed his other hand on her large bag and returned the hat to his head. "Good to see you, Sarah." His baritone voice seeped under her skin.

Darn. It might have been better not to see him up close.

Just as she remembered, his dark hair was still cropped short to keep him cool as he worked the farm. With his hat back on his head, no stray curls escaped. A five o'clock shadow of a beard highlighted the strong facial structure he'd had as an eighteen-year-old. Now in its maturity the chiseled features spoke of hard work and a wariness she didn't remember from the past. The tension flexing that very jaw implied he was as uncertain about seeing her as she was of him.

"Thanks." She finally managed to find her voice. She picked up the guitar case, happy to let him manage the large, unwieldy case of clothes. The worn wheels were uneven and one of them occasionally fell off if it hit a bump. Maneuvering it in a straight line would be a chore.

"I'll lead," he said. "The truck is parked in the back forty. The parking lot was pretty full."

She was glad he didn't expect conversation and that he walked in front. It would give her a chance to scan the rest of him. She shouldn't —she knew that. She was an idiot for even caring what he looked like. After all, he'd not only broken her heart when he'd run off with Amanda, but he completely disappeared without giving her a chance to properly break-up with him.

The years should've healed that particular hurt. She needed to get to a place where she could appreciate his physicality like she would a good horse or a prize bull. No need to get her heart involved at all.

Her gaze slid downward.

Her heart might be out of the picture, but her pulse was right there with her. Tom Pawlak had a rugged, gorgeous aspect that reminded her of the Marlboro Man of her childhood. The one plastered across billboards throughout the south—only minus the cigarette. Tom still screamed dark and dangerous. Dressed in faded jeans and dark brown cowboy boots, he looked every bit the handsome cowboy. A dark blue, close fitting T-shirt strained across a broad, muscled chest that appeared even stronger than she remembered. The worn brown leather jacket hung open to just below his waist, accentuating the fit of his jeans as he gave up on rolling her case and easily lifted it while striding through the parking lot. Oh, yeah, this was the Tom she remembered except a little harder, muscles better defined, definitely a man and not a boy.

Sarah couldn't help but wonder what had become of that boy after she left. The boy who had been her best friend and then became the love of her life when they began dating her junior year of high school. The same boy-man who she had decided, against her own religious beliefs, would take her virginity. She was so sure they loved each other. She was so sure they would be married right out of high school, that she wasn't even conflicted about the decision.

They had planned to meet graduation night and she was ready. Sarah had waited for four hours for him to show at the barn that night. She had prepared the perfect scene in the hayloft—a soft white sheet spread over the hay and strewn with rose petals. It was a scene to rival any romance novel she'd ever read. She'd even obtained a condom from her best friend who had spent a giggly graduation morning training her how to put it over a banana.

After two weeks of her wondering if he'd died or been kidnapped, he'd rolled into town with Amanda in his truck. To make matters worse, Amanda wasted no time prancing around town talking up the great sex that could be had with the bad boy of Broken Bow—his endurance, his virility, how many times and ways they had done it over the past two weeks. She particularly seemed to take pains to bring it up within earshot of Sarah.

Tom had never searched for Sarah to explain or to even attempt an apology. Instead, he worked his way through every rich girl who wanted to make it with the young stud of Broken Bow.

That was when she decided she had to leave. She couldn't imagine staying in the same small town knowing that there was a good likelihood every girl in town who wanted to, except Sarah, had made it with Tom. Whenever she walked into the grocery store, she could feel eyes following her. She could hear the whispers behind her back. "That's poor Sarah. She actually loved him." She couldn't even go to the feed store without the cowboys there staring at her. When even hard-edged cowboys pity you, it is best to get out of town.

She packed everything and headed west. She'd had no plan, no destination. It took six days to purge Tom's betrayal from her system, and on the seventh day she landed in Portland, Oregon.

Sarah stopped watching him walk. She berated herself for even noticing. Maybe she wasn't as immune as she'd thought. Remembering those days would do nothing to help her face the next few months with her father. She would have to work hard to make sure she and Tom Pawlak rarely crossed paths on the farm.

TOM HEAVED the large case into the bed of the truck. "I assume you want to hang on to the guitar."

"Yes, it's too fragile to let it bounce around in the back of your truck."

He pointed to the case. "I can slide it behind the seat. Is that okay?"

She nodded and he reached for it, his fingers sliding over hers to grasp the handle. She quickly pulled her hand away as if it had been burned. He ground his teeth together.

Tom held the door for her to climb in. She scooted past him and leveraged herself onto the seat without even a brush of clothing between them. "Thank you," she said, her eyes straight ahead.

He frowned and pushed the door closed just a little too hard. He turned and looked out over the parking lot. Stomping to the other side of the truck and slamming the door would solve nothing. Is this what it was going to be like every time they ran into each other at her house? Going out of her way not to talk, not to stand close enough to even brush against each other?

He rounded the hood with long, confident strides, opened the door and slid onto the bench seat. He reached across her lap, purposefully brushing his forearm against her leg as he opened the glove compartment to retrieve his sunglasses. She pulled in her chest and stomach, burying her spine as far as possible into the seat back.

"Dammit, Sarah!" He slammed the glove compartment closed. "I'm not going to jump your bones. I'm not even going to make a play for you. But we can't work together on the farm, take care of your father, or share cooking if you can't stand an occasional touch now and then."

He watched her chest rise and fall as she took a deep breath. She clasped her hands tight in her lap and stared forward, as if even turning to face him was too painful.

"Given our past together," she began, her voice like that of a schoolmarm disciplining the students. "I think it's best that we make up a schedule to ensure our paths don't cross very often. In fact, now that I'm here to care for my father, we don't need to see each other at all except in emergency situations. You can be in charge of the farm and I'll be in charge of the house."

Tom turned the key in the ignition and backed out of the parking space. He didn't speak as he threw away one angry response after the other. Once he turned on the highway he'd calmed a bit.

"You have it all worked out don't you?" He glanced to the side in time to see her stiffen again.

"Well, no...I just think that would be best."

"Why?"

She squirmed in her seat. "Well...because...I..."

"Are you afraid that being around me will make you love me again?"

She whipped her head around and faced him head on. "Absolutely not! There is nothing, nothing you could ever do again to make me love you. Get that out of your head Tom Pawlak. Right now! Nothing!"

Tom chuckled. "Uh huh."

"Don't you laugh at me! I…just…can't…" She turned her face toward the window and her shoulders sagged.

He'd heard the tears in her throat when she couldn't finish that sentence. His hand twitched on the steering wheel, wanting to reach for her, to comfort her. Instead, he held tight to the steering wheel and concentrated on the traffic straight ahead.

"I'm sorry," he said after a couple minutes passed. "I didn't mean to laugh. I know it's hard seeing me again. Believe me, it's hard for me too." He glanced to the side. Her head now leaned on the window.

"It's just that it's not going to be so easy to avoid each other. Your father is very ill. One day, he'll seem like his old self, walking around the house, giving orders, drinking like a fish."

She raised her head from the window. "He's still drinking?" she asked, not as a question but more in resignation to the inevitable.

"Yes. I suspect his last act before he dies will be to take one last drink of whisky."

She let out a sigh. "I guess I know that. I always knew that drinking would kill him or someone else."

His hands twitched on the steering wheel. He again pushed back the desire to touch her, to comfort her.

After a long silence, she turned slightly toward him. "And the other days? The days when he's not himself?"

"Never mind," Tom said. "There will be plenty of time to talk about this. You have enough to worry about right now. Why don't you take a rest. I'll wake you when we get to the farm."

"No. I want to know. I want to know what I'm in for."

He looked at her for a moment, then turned his attention back to the road. It was easier to talk without worrying about her reaction. It was a good thing he was driving.

"A lot of days he can barely get out of bed, especially if he had a hard day of drinking and remembering. On those days, I'm the one who bathes him, cleans him up when he can't get to the bathroom, brings in his meals."

"I didn't realize. I guess I thought maybe he had a nurse or something."

"Hospice offered him a nurse, but you know your dad. He said the only reason to have a nurse is if she wanted to have sex with him. There was no way he was having some stranger taking care of him. Truth is he barely tolerates me doing it."

"Thank you, Tom." She folded her hands in her lap. "I'm sorry I acted like such an idiot before. Now I understand that we will see each other a lot more than I planned. It's just hard. Hard to be back."

Several seconds ticked away in silence before she spoke again. "You know my relationship with my father has never been a good one. Coming here, giving up my career for a month or more, seeing you, it's just—

"A lot to take on," he said.

She nodded. "Yes." She took another deep breath. "I have friends, a home, a career that I love, all of it two thousand miles away from here. I know how to act there. I know that I'm accepted for who I am." She turned back to the window. "I don't have the baggage of being alcoholic Jack's poor daughter, or that poor girl who was too naïve to know her boyfriend was screwing everyone in town except her."

That stung. Tom drove in silence.

Tom had no illusions of starting a romantic relationship with her again. That ship had sailed and sunk to the bottom of the ocean never to be resurrected. He understood he screwed up royally seven years ago. But they were both different people now. Why couldn't they just be friends? Was that too much too ask?

"Let's just take it one day at a time," he finally said. "No promises. No expectations. Let's just focus on your dad and the farm. Okay?"

"I can do that," she said. "I can do that," she said again, her voice a whisper as if she was trying to convince herself.

Tom pulled the truck into the drive in front of the house with Sarah sound asleep, her head propped on his shoulder. He remembered several evenings bringing her home after a football game and she'd be sleeping this way.

Without thinking, he brushed his lips across the top of her head just like he always had before. "Sarah, we're here." He gently pushed her shoulders away from him. "Sarah, you're home."

She stirred next to him but didn't come fully awake. "Home? Are Theresa and Kat inside? I'm so tired. I'm not sure I can find my key."

Theresa and Kat? She must be talking about her Oregon friends. "You're in Broken Bow. We're at your father's place."

Sarah opened her eyes wide, stared absently at Tom, then scanned the car as if trying to orient herself. "Oh. Did I fall asleep? That was fast. We're here then." Her voice tensed and it was up at least half an octave. "I guess we need to get inside. I'll get my stuff. Oh my goodness. I was lost there for a minute. I wasn't sure where I was." She reached for the handle but struggled to figure it out.

Tom turned her toward him, his hands strong on her shoulders. "Deep breaths. It's going to be okay."

She stiffened under his touch and he withdrew. "No. It's not. It will never be okay again. But I'll make it work. I'll get through this, and then I'll get to go home." She tried the door once more and it opened easily.

Tom jumped out of his side of the truck and took the luggage out of the back before she could get to it. By the time he got to her side of the door, she'd already retrieved her guitar case.

Like a martyr facing the gallows, she stood tall and stared at the front door of the house. "Let's do this." She strode to the porch, knocked and waited.

A dog barked wildly from inside the house.

"Go away!" Her father's voice shouted from the inside. "Whatever you've got I don't want it."

Tom unlocked the door with his key. "Jack, put the safety on the gun. It's me and I have Sarah with me."

"Gun?" Sarah shivered.

Tom pushed the door open and her father staggered into the hall, a pistol in his hand.

~

"SARAH?" He wrapped his arms around her. She couldn't help but stiffen in his arms. She held back the need to retch from the smell of his clothes. It was as if he had taken a bath in whisky about a week ago, clothes and all. Out of the corner of her eye, she saw Tom remove the gun, check the safety and then put it in a drawer.

The dog barked and ran in circles around her and her father.

"Hi, Dad," she said, as she managed to extricate herself from his awkward embrace.

She bent to the dog and scratched him behind the ears. "Your still here, Kip. How have you been?"

"Great." Her Dad's low voice boomed. "I'm dying but that's nothing new. It's just closer this time. I have a timeline. Doc says three months. I'm trying to beat the clock."

She wasn't sure how to respond. She didn't know what he really meant. She kept petting Kip. At least she knew the dog still loved her.

"Cat got your tongue, missy?" He gestured toward the kitchen. "Come in, let's have a drink together, celebrate your homecoming."

"Uh, I don't drink, Dad. Remember?"

"That's all right!" He slapped her on the back. "I'll drink for both of us. You want coffee? Water? I think that's all I have to offer. Is that right Tom?"

"There's also juice and milk, and I have sandwich makings too. I'll get it ready. You two visit. You still like ham and cheese?"

Sarah nodded. Nothing had really changed. She had no expectation that it would, exactly, but she'd hoped—or maybe she had just refused to think about it.

CHAPTER 4

S ARAH CRINGED AS HER FATHER POURED two shots of whisky into his glass, drank it in one gulp and then poured another two shots. Then he staggered the few feet to the table and sat down in the chair across from her.

For the first time she could see how much he had changed in the last seven years. Whereas before he'd been overweight and rosy-cheeked, almost like Santa, now he was half the size of his former self. His skin had a yellow cast to it. Even the whites of his eyes looked buttery. Small, red, spider-like veins crawled across his nose and cheeks. It was as if he'd aged twenty years instead of seven.

"How about ham and cheese for you, Jack?" Tom asked.

"Nope. This is my lunch."

"Something else, maybe? Turkey? Soup?"

"I said no," Jack yelled. "You know I don't eat until dinner." He tapped on his glass. "This is it. This is everything I need."

"Dad?" Sarah drew out the name like she did when she was a child. "Please have something to eat. It can't be good to go all day without food."

"Nothing's good for me anymore, Sarah." He took a long draught. "This is all I have now. Courage, comfort, and love all rolled into one."

Sarah wanted to shout, *You have me!* But she didn't. She used to do that as child. It didn't work then and it certainly wouldn't work now.

"You know that refusing to eat, just drinking will only rush your death, right?"

"That's exactly what I'm doing, little girl. The quicker I'm out of here the better for everyone. Tom there keeps taking the bullets out of my guns, otherwise I'd do it tomorrow now that you're here to take over this place."

Sarah focused on the window that had a view out to the barn. It was worse than she'd imagined. At least when she was young, there were brief periods of sobriety—or at least he tried to act like there was something as important as drinking. But now clearly nothing else was important. How dare he threaten to shoot himself. That was manipulative and selfish. And here she was acting like that same scared little girl who had run away from home.

She clenched her teeth and narrowed her eyes, then looked back at her father. "You've done a good job of ensuring your death already. And there is nothing I can do to stop you from drinking."

"Got that right," her father said as he stood to pour another.

"But I swear, if you do something like shoot yourself I absolutely will not stay here. I will not take care of the house. I will not take care of the farm. I'll sell it for pennies just to be done with it. I didn't come all this way—away from my friends, away from a family that actually loves me—to spend what little time I have cleaning up your bloody mess like I would a slaughtered pig to take to the meat processing facility."

Her father laughed long and hard.

"My little girl grew a backbone after all." He reached over and covered her hands with his, but she withdrew them. "And don't you think I don't love you. I love you more than any thing in this world. I'm your family—your only family, for better or worse. I know that since your mama died I'm the worst father ever, but that doesn't mean I don't love you."

Sarah shook so hard with a combination of anger and regret that she couldn't respond. As if knowing she was upset, Kip stirred from under the table and nuzzled her knee.

She clenched her mouth closed lest she said what she actually felt—how everything he did since her mother died was as if he was purposefully trampling on her grave. She would never believe he loved her. He only cared about himself, *his* hurt, *his* pain, *his* needs. He never cared about hers. If he really loved her, really cared about her, he wouldn't drink himself into a coma and make threats about committing suicide. No, that is why she ran away. The thing he loved most in his life was his whisky, not his daughter. It was obvious nothing had changed.

Tom placed the ham and cheese sandwich in front of her, and then sat across from her with his own plate. He'd grilled it and the cheese oozed out of the side, just the way she liked it. The problem was she didn't feel like eating now. As usual, her father had ruined what little enjoyment she could have had from simply eating a good sandwich. Now that she saw him this way, she could barely face the fact that she had to spend the next three months reliving her childhood just so she could say she honored her father on his deathbed.

"Is something wrong with the sandwich?" Tom asked. "Did I cook it wrong."

"No." Sarah said on a sigh. "I think I'm just tired from the trip. That's all." She forced herself to take a small bite and then put it down. She pasted a smile on her face. "Thanks Tom. It's delicious. Really."

There the three sat. No one talking, and Sarah sneaking parts of her sandwhich to Kip under the table.

She studied Tom, then moved to her father. It was as if everyone knew the situation was hopeless, that her coming here was a big mistake, but no one had the guts to say it—especially her. In her mind, she was half way out the door, suitcase in hand, unable to face all of this drama again. Tom continued to eat like a robot. Her father was on his fourth drink and could barely sit at the table. It was all she could do to force herself to take another bite. After the third bite she gave up and pushed the plate away.

Tom looked up and raised an eyebrow.

She shook her head. It required a concentration of all her energy not to cry. Or scream. Or run. There was no way she could eat.

Tom stood and took her plate. "Shall I give the rest of this to the dog?"

She nodded and Tom put the plate on the floor just to the right of the sink. He whistled and Kip moved from under the table and snarfed up the remains.

"It's been a long day. If you want to go get set up in your room, go ahead."

She nodded, then stood and moved like a ghost toward her bedroom. She couldn't think right now, couldn't accept that she was back in the exact same environment she left seven years ago. Her father hadn't changed. In fact he'd gotten worse. The house was still a wreck, even though it appeared that Tom had done some work on it. Then there was Tom—the one man she swore she'd never see again. And here he was right in the middle of her life again. She was so confused. So tired.

When she opened the door, it was the last straw. It was as if she'd just graduated from high school. The paint colors were the same. The baby blue vanity and mirror were in the same place, along with the shredded picture of Tom she had removed from the mirror and torn into tiny pieces onto the vanity top before packing her suitcase and running out the door. The vanity was covered with a thin layer of dust. She wouldn't be surprised if the sheets hadn't been changed since she left seven years ago.

Sarah got on her knees next to the bed and rested her head in her palms. Lord, what have I gotten myself into? She prayed silently, as tears streamed onto the bed. I don't know why I'm here, what I should do. I want to honor my father but I don't know how. I can't find anything in him to honor. Am I required to be here just because his seed impregnated my mother?

She didn't know how long she was on her knees, asking question after question until she couldn't even form questions any more. After a long pause she rose and started unpacking. She put clothes in the closet. Checked the chest of drawers. They smelled as if they'd just been cleaned. She even sniffed the bed sheets. Yes, they smelled fresh too. Was that Tom's doing? Probably. Maybe he was different now. Maybe he was at least a little responsible.

With everything in its place, she finally undressed, changed into her PJs and slipped between the covers. Whisky hadn't always been his focus, she finally admitted to herself. There had been good times before her mother died. She'd focus on that. She'd honor that part of him.

She turned off the light on the bedstand and fell instantly asleep.

TOM FINISHED hand washing the dishes with one eye on Jack. There had been many nights when Jack got drunk so fast that he simply fell out of his chair onto the floor. He was afraid this would be one of those nights. Though he longed to go down the hall and comfort Sarah, he knew this was just as hard for Jack. It brought back memories Jack had worked hard to suppress. Those resurrected memories included plenty of regrets—regrets that he tried to drink away tonight.

"Jack, let's get you to bed, okay?" Tom shook Jack's shoulder when there was no response. "Come on, Jack. You know I can't carry you. If you don't at least stand and try to walk, I'll have to drag you down the hall." He shook Jack again.

"What?" Jack said, obviously disoriented. "What?"

"Time for bed," Tom repeated.

"Where's Sarah? Where's my kiss good night from my little girl?" Jack rose on wobbly legs and turned toward Sarah's room.

"That wouldn't be a good idea," Tom said, gently steering him in the opposite direction.

"Why not? I want to tell her I'm sorry. I want to tell her I do love her."

"Not tonight," Tom said, urging Jack through the kitchen and to the other side of the house where the master bedroom was located. "You can tell her tomorrow."

"What did I say?" Jack asked. "What did I do to make her run?"

Tom opened the bedroom door and pushed Jack inside toward the bed. "We both did bad things. If one of us had been a good man, she might have stayed. But both of us being jackasses was too much."

Jack flopped onto the bed, his eyes focused on the ceiling. "I've been an ass all my life," he said. "I was drinking too much already in high school. Even when I met Lizzie I was drinking, but she married me anyway. Why did Lizzie marry me, Tom? I never understood that."

"Beats me," Tom said as he pulled Jack's shirt over his head and then got to work on getting the rest of him undressed and into pajamas. "Certainly not for your good looks."

Jack snorted. "I wasn't always old and crotchety, you know."

"Yeah. I've seen the pictures."

"Of Lizzie and me? She was so beautiful. I couldn't believe how lucky I was. But even with her I couldn't stop drinking. I cut back a little … well at least most of the time."

Tom finally had Jack undressed. "Want to use the facilities before I get the pajamas on you?"

"No." Then Jack stood. "Yes." He ambled into the bathroom, bouncing off the wall closest to the door before making it inside.

Tom readied the pajamas on the bed. He heard the toilet flush and Jack emerged, leaning against the wall as if he couldn't take another step.

"I've tried to stop," Jack slurred as he slowly inched his way back to the bed. "I told Lizzie I would. I even went to AA for a couple of weeks. But I couldn't do it. I just kept thinking if I was man enough I could stop on my own. Then I'd try. Then I'd fail. Then I'd go to another meeting. Then …"

Jack fell onto the bed and went instantly to sleep. Tom struggled with the dead weight to get pajama pants on him and get him under the covers. He wasn't going to leave him naked, like he did some nights, because Jack occasionally woke up and wandered around the house not knowing where he was. The last thing Sarah needed was her father to appear in her bedroom naked and confused.

"Good night, Jack," Tom said as he turned off the light.

"I'm sorry, Lizzie." Jack's voice cracked and Tom could hear the tears. "I'm so sorry. Please forgive me." Then he sobbed into his pillow.

Tom sighed. Some drunks became violent like his dad, other drunks acted like they were invincible and did stupid things like drive fast or jump into raging rivers. But Jack became maudlin. He relived all his regrets and that usually made him drink even more to erase them—at least temporarily.

Within a few weeks of returning to Broken Bow, Tom swore off alcohol. He hadn't become an alcoholic … yet. But he'd been traveling that path, trying to erase his fears and boost his confidence. Tom saw firsthand that you couldn't ever drink enough to forget permanently and that the confidence you felt was transitory at best. Jack taught him that, whether he meant to or not.

CHAPTER 5

ARAH WOKE WITH THE SUNRISE. She glanced around her childhood room and cringed. As soon as she had a few moments, she was cleaning this from top to bottom. The first thing to go would be everything on the dressing table. It would be the first step to sweeping Tom out of her life.

She knew how to work the farm. She'd done it all her life growing up, especially after her mother died. Dad couldn't be counted on to do anything, so Sarah had done enough to keep food on the table. Getting outside to work in the field would help take her mind off why she was here and how confused she was inside.

Emotions of gratitude and resentment warred inside her. She appreciated Tom's taking care of her father. If he hadn't stepped up to help, Sarah wouldn't even know about her father dying. And it did seem that Tom was a comfort to her father, not to mention he did all kinds of things Sarah couldn't imagine doing like bathing and dressing him.

Yet, she couldn't understand what he was doing here. Didn't he have better things to do with his time than spend his days with a cranky alcoholic and a subsistence farm? Surely he had a life of his own.

She showered quickly in the hall bath, then dressed in jeans and sturdy socks. After a stop in the kitchen for coffee, she'd put on her boots and get out into the field early. Breakfast always came after finishing the morning chores. One of her best memories of her childhood was watching the sun rise over the rows of vegetables. She remembered drawing out the chickens outside to feed so she could go in and check for fresh eggs.

She tiptoed down the hall in her stocking feet to the kitchen. She let out a breath of relief when she saw the light was not on. Good. She wouldn't be running into Tom just yet.

The smell of freshly brewed coffee greeted her as she stepped into the kitchen. Next to the stove, the light on the coffeemaker glowed like a beacon in the darkness of the room. As quietly as possible she extracted a coffee cup from the cupboard and filled it with strong, black coffee. Sarah had learned to drink coffee black when she was a teenager, as she could never count on Dad to buy sugar or milk. In fact, she could never count on Dad to buy anything except whisky.

She took her time savoring that first cup and the quiet around her. Closing her eyes for just a moment she imagined how it was when her mother was alive. She would already be up, cooking eggs and bacon, and pancakes with butter and syrup to get Sarah off to school with a full stomach.

While Sarah was at school, her mother would be at a job in town. She did books for OK Insurance, a company that specialized in insuring small farmers—what some people called suitcase farmers or sidewalk farmers. Most small farmers were hobbyists—gentleman farmers who bought property to keep horses and perhaps grow a few vegetables to sell at local farmers markets. Only a few family farms were left. To survive, at least one person had to work outside of the farm.

Dad used to say they were farmers because it was in their blood. His father was a farmer and his grandfather was a farmer. Sarah believed they were farmers because her father could continue to drink. He'd tried to get a job off the farm and the longest he lasted was three months. That was when he worked for a brewery. Everyone there drank, so it took longer than usual for the management to realize he was an alcoholic and couldn't stay on task in the long run.

Sarah shook her head. She had to stop thinking about her father's failures. It would make her time here too miserable. She finished up her first cup of coffee and then poured another cup into a Thermos. Out the kitchen window, she could see the sky getting lighter. Sunrise. She hurried to put on her boots and a rain slicker.

Her boots felt sturdy and warm as she walked slowly toward the chicken coop with Kip trying to herd her. A mist hung over the field and, as the first rays of sunshine peeked from behind a cloud, a small rainbow touched one end of the field. It was as if God was blessing the crops.

"God's promise," Tom said behind her.

She gasped and dropped her thermos. She hadn't heard him come from anywhere. Kip ran circles around them.

Tom quickly bent to retrieve it. "I'm sorry. I didn't mean to startle you. Are you okay?" He brushed the dirt off the Thermos and handed it back to her. When she took it their fingers touched and he held them there for a moment. A tingling sensation went right up her arm.

"I'm fine." Breathless, Sarah yanked the cup away and took a step back.

His smile crinkled the corners of his blue-grey eyes. "I didn't know I had such a dramatic effect on you,"

She snorted. "You don't." Maybe he did, but she wasn't going to let him know that. "I see you still have an ego. I'm not one of your rich girls asking to be seduced. Still chasing anything in a skirt?"

He frowned and looked away for a moment. Then his spine stiffened and he turned to look straight into her eyes. "I'm not the man you left seven years ago, Sarah. I'm sorry I hurt you. I wish I could take it back and start over, but I can't. We can only start from today."

She tried to look anywhere but at him. It did no good. Her gaze stayed on his face, a compulsion she couldn't deny. He smelled of fresh cut hay and spearmint gum. Memories flooded her—him walking her home after the prom, his strong arm wrapped around her waist; him holding her face, just like she wished he would now, and gently kiss her.

Sarah stepped backward a couple feet and scuffed her boot in the dirt, shaking her head. "We are not starting anything, Tom Pawlak. I don't care who you are now. I don't want to know anything about you."

"I want to know all about you, Sarah," he countered. "I want to know what you've been doing in Portland, Oregon. I want to know what kinds of songs you write. I want to hear you play your guitar and sing. I want to know what you believe and what you don't believe. I want to know everything."

She swallowed, searching for her voice. She'd brought her guitar, but it was as if her past had taken over and she couldn't escape it. A large shadow loomed in her head, blotting out the music she had always had inside her. She could barely even remember the melody line to the song she'd been so excited about when she left Portland. Though the last two lines of the chorus were stuck in her head. *Lead me through the muddy dark. Help me mend this broken heart.*

She drew her lower lip beneath her teeth, then released it. "You don't always get what you want," she said, pushing her shoulders back and standing tall. "That's all you need to know about me, Tom Pawlak. You can't have me. You missed your chance and there is no way I'm going there again."

She turned away from him and walked directly to the chicken coop, Kip followed barking at her with every step.

"I already collected the eggs," Tom yelled after her.

She stopped in her tracks. Why was he making it so darn difficult to escape? Was it his purpose in life to make her miserable … again?

She turned back to him, her fist clenched hard around the Thermos. "What is it you want, Tom?"

"I told you, I want to know who you are … now."

"No. I mean why are you really here? Why are you taking care of my father, a man you barely knew and who is as ungrateful as they come. What are you looking to get out of this? The house? Well you can have it. You don't have to pretend to be nice to me. On my oath, I'll sign it over to you upon his death. I'll never stay here. There are too many bad memories. As soon as Dad is gone, I'm out of here. I don't care what you do with the house, the farm, any of it. Just leave me alone."

She was shaking now, wobbling between anger and loss—loss of all things she'd wanted when she believed in love conquering all. When she believed she could stop her mother from dying if she only prayed harder. When she believed she could save her father from alcoholism if she was only a better daughter. When she believed she could marry Tom, if only—

"Just leave me alone," she said again. "Leave me alone."

She turned and ran toward the farthest fence in the field.

Sarah returned to the house after several hours of walking and praying—just trying to make sense of it all. At one point, she had sat for so long that Kip fell asleep at her feet.

She purposely waited until after the usual lunch hour so she wouldn't run into Tom again. She knew she couldn't avoid him forever, but she needed to figure out how to not let her emotions get the better of her every time they ran into each other.

"Your father would like to see you." This time she heard him coming down the hall to the kitchen. "He's in pretty rough shape today. I don't think he'll be getting out of bed."

For a moment her heart skipped a beat at the thought her father might die sooner than the three months the doctor's suggested. Then she remembered this was her father. "Rough shape, as in drunk already?" she asked. "Or as in he's getting worse."

Tom looked at her unblinking. There was a sadness to his stare. Did he think she was heartless? Not worried about her dad? Good if he did. Maybe it would make sure he didn't try to get back in a relationship.

"He's physically worse." Tom stepped to the cupboard near her chair. On the top shelf were several pill bottles. He retrieved four of them and took a pill out of each one. "The disease is moving faster than anyone anticipated," he said as he poured a glass of water and then gathered the pills into a small paper cup.

"It's hard to tell the difference." Sarah cringed at her words.

Tom remained silent.

What was wrong with her? Since she arrived she'd turned into different person. Her Sweetwater Canyon family wouldn't recognize this Sarah. Unforgiving. Mean.

"I'm sorry," Sarah said. "It seems that being here brings out the worst in me."

"It's hard to face your past." Tom lightly placed a hand on her shoulder. "I know. I've spent the last few years trying to make amends throughout town."

"But I've done nothing wrong," Sarah said. "Why do I have to forgive him? He should be the one asking me for forgiveness."

Tom shrugged his shoulders "We all do things we're ashamed of. We all need to ask forgiveness sometimes."

He moved out of the kitchen with the water and the pills. "You might as well come now if you're going to talk to your father today. After taking these pills, it will be about twenty minutes before he falls asleep again. Then it will be five or six hours before he wakes."

She followed Tom to her father's room. She waited outside the door while Tom gave him his medicine and took care of his personal needs. It seemed like a long time. Then she heard Tom asking Jack if he wanted to speak with her. She couldn't hear what was mumbled. Finally, Tom appeared at the door.

"You can go in now. He's not very coherent. The pain has been especially bad today, so he's had more than the usual amount of morphine."

"Morphine?" She hadn't realized it was that bad.

"He has a pump. He can press it when he's in pain. Of course it will only administer so much, so he can't overdose."

How much more didn't she know? She'd been so wrapped up in

her own reaction to coming here that she hadn't really thought about her father's disease.

"Why doesn't he have the kind of pump they implant? What if he pulls out the I.V.?"

"The implanted pump requires surgery and it requires a diagnosis of at least six months to live and a patient who has been stabilized on oral medication."

Sarah chuckled ruefully. "Stability is a word my father doesn't know." She stared at the door. "Does this mean he's dying more quickly than thought?"

"It's hard to know." Tom hung his head. "The three months was a best-case scenario—if he stopped drinking and did everything the doctor's suggested."

"Of course that didn't happen." Sarah couldn't keep the anger out of her voice.

"No." Tom gently turned her toward him and held her gaze. "Sarah, he's going to die like he lived. That's all he can do. He made his choices and now he is paying a price for that. At least he's not a hypocrite, turning to religion at the last moment—not because he believes but just in case."

Sarah's eyes widened. Tom didn't believe. She didn't remember that about him. But then, given all that happened, did she ever really know him? Did he believe anything at all? Had he ever prayed for her father to live?

She shook her head. She didn't have time to figure out what Tom did or didn't believe. If her father would be asleep inside twenty minutes she needed to get in there.

"I'm sorry I haven't been asking more questions," she said. "I do want to know what's happened and what to expect. Can we talk later?"

"Tomorrow." Tom said. "I have to get to work now."

"Work? You have another job besides the farm?"

Tom nodded.

"But how? Why?"

He waved his hand to stop her. "Tomorrow. I'll tell you tomorrow." Then he left her standing in the hall at her father's door.

Lord, I don't know if I can do this, she prayed. I don't want him to die thinking I hate him. But I can't forgive him. I know I should, but I can't. Please help me do what's right.

She turned the knob and walked in.

A low lamp was on next to the bed. Her father was propped up on pillows with his eyes closed. Somehow he seemed even worse than yesterday. He still had that jaundiced look, but his skin was paler now, almost translucent.

"Daddy?" She kept her voice low in case he was already asleep.

His eyes opened slowly. "Sarah?"

She crossed and took his hand. "Yes, Daddy. I'm here."

He squeezed her hand. "Come closer. Sit on the edge of the bed so I can see you."

She did, not letting go of his hand.

"Sarah, I have to talk to you. I don't have much longer and I have so much to tell you."

Her eyes filled. She wanted to tell him he could beat this, that she would do whatever it took to get him to better doctors, better hospitals. But she knew he would never go. He'd given up on both of their lives more than fifteen years ago when her mother died. There was no way he would stay around now.

"Sarah?" he asked again after nodding off for a minute.

"Yes, I'm still here."

"I'm sorry. I'm sorry I wasn't there for you."

She swallowed hard. She'd been wanting to hear this all her life; and here it was just like in the movies. An act of contrition just before he died.

"I wasn't there for you when your mother died and I completely left you after that. The truth is I didn't believe I could live without Lizzie. The only reason I didn't follow her then and there was because of you. I didn't want you to be without any parent. I didn't want you in the state system."

"I...I..." She couldn't find words. She couldn't help but wonder if maybe she would have been better off in a foster home than trying all those years to save her father from himself.

"I don't expect you to forgive me, Sarah. I don't deserve your forgiveness. I just want you to know I never stopped loving you. I never stopped wanting the best life possible for you. I know I wasn't there when you needed me most, but I loved you still."

"Daddy, I don't know what to say. I...I'm confused. I'm scared. I don't want you to die."

"I know, sweetheart. I know." Then he nodded off.

She sat there for a few minutes waiting for him to wake up again. It hadn't been twenty minutes. Not even close. She moved to withdraw her hand but he held tight, so she stayed. She wasn't sure if he was awake or asleep. But he evidently wanted her to stay. At least she could do that.

"Daddy, I'm sorry too," she whispered. "I wasn't there for you either. I just didn't understand your grief. I didn't understand that drinking was an addiction. I hope you can forgive me."

His hand slipped away. There was no response.

She cried silently. Tom was right. She needed forgiveness too. She had spent so much time being angry about what she didn't get from her father, that she never considered what he might need. All those years of anger, all those years of wanting a dad who would take care of her and play with her, be there when she went to the prom, be someone she could count on. But he hadn't been and her reaction had been anger. The truth was he couldn't take care of himself, so how could he have taken care of her?

If only she hadn't ignored him the last two years. If only she had made contact, she would have known about this diagnosis. She could have come home and at least visited, or … or? She hoped she would have come home and found a way to repair their relationship sooner. Now, there was no time. Now, there would never be the chance at a real relationship.

She stood and watched her father's labored breathing. He was so frail, so sick. He'd always been sick. She just didn't see it before.

She shook her head as she moved toward the door. Please don't let him die until I work this out, she prayed. Please don't let this be his last day.

Her hands reached for the doorknob and she turned it slowly. When she stepped into the hall she left the door cracked. She would sleep on the couch tonight in case he called out, in case he needed help.

CHAPTER 6

*T*HE ALARM WOKE TOM AT SEVEN. He rolled over and groaned. He'd crashed so hard last night that he didn't even take his clothes off before hitting the bed. He had a headache and a sore shoulder from sleeping in a funny position. He probably didn't move all night. Coffee. Must have coffee. But first he needed to shower and change.

He wasn't sure how much longer he could do this. Before Jack became so ill, he could manage all his chores at the farm and still do forty hours a week at his night job and get a good five to six hours of sleep. But this past month it wasn't working out that way. If he managed three hours of sleep on a regular basis, he was lucky. Tom knew that as Jack got worse he'd need to spend even more time with him. More medications, more monitoring, more taking care of his every need. He knew the end was near, just not how close. Could be a few days or another month. Should he ask for leave now or wait a little longer?

He groaned again and forced himself out of bed. He stripped off yesterday's clothes as he headed for the shower. When he was dressed, he'd grab some coffee at the house, check on Jack, and try not to run into Sarah before he got back out the door to start on chores.

Tom had managed to get the broccoli, cabbage, beets, and cauliflower in the ground last week. Today he needed to get the kale, lettuce and onions in. By the end of the week, the rest of the early spring planting had to be done. With the farm not even covering its cost, the entire forty acres was impossible to manage. Tom planted crops in five-acre plots, then rotated them each year to make sure the soil wasn't depleted.

When he first took over for Jack, he'd implemented no-till, organic farming with a diversity of vegetables instead of planting only two or three crops. It took away some of the costs in renting machines to do the work, but then it increased his labor. It fit the need for subsistence farming and food first, and still left enough crops to capitalize on the growth in demand for organic produce. The late start today would make it difficult to get all the seed he wanted in today while also checking on Jack.

Nothing he could do about it. Just had to keep putting one foot in front of the other and get it done. He turned on the shower and let the hot water massage his tired body as he prepared for the day ahead.

TOM QUIETLY UNLOCKED the front door and stepped into the dark living room. He stopped in his tracks to the kitchen. Kip dropped from the sofa and dashed out the front door before he closed it.

There was Sarah, on the couch, sleeping on her side, her rear end snuggled into the back of the sofa. Her right foot peeked out from the bottom of the blanket. His mouth hung open, but he didn't breathe, didn't blink. If only he had been a better man seven years ago, he might be waking up beside her now. He could be enjoying watching her sleep every morning.

He reached toward her face to gently move a lock of hair out of her eyes. He stopped. What was he thinking? No touching. That would only take him down a path with no good ending. She'd made it clear there was no chance for a relationship and he didn't blame her.

But he couldn't help standing and just taking her in, catching her in an uncontrolled moment where there were no masks of fear or distrust. The blanket had slipped to her waist and he moved it back to her shoulders. She wore a sky blue, v-neck T-shirt that rose and fell with every breath that escaped in a quiet whisper between her lips. He still remembered tasting those lips all those years ago. With each kiss he'd become more scared. Scared of her all encompassing love. Scared that he loved her beyond reason. He remembered the delicate layers of her lips and her mouth able to express her myriad of emotions in just one kiss.

Back then, he didn't know what to do with that kind of love and trust. He didn't deserve it and he didn't believe it could last. So he ran —ran from the pain he knew would come later when she realized he could never be her prince in shining armor. He didn't know how. He had no role model for marriage, for being a good husband, even for being a good man.

The intervening years taught him how to be a good man. Now he was capable. But it was too late for him and Sarah.

Her tense forehead showed worry lines even in her sleep. He wished he could wipe those lines away. He wished that he could bring her peace and some respite from all that was to come with her father. Most of all, he hated that his mere presence added more worry to her already full plate.

He wiped a fist across his moist eyes. Best get that coffee and get out of here before he did something he'd regret. He took one last glimpse of her beautiful sleeping form and then turned to the kitchen without looking back.

SARAH FILLED two thermoses with coffee and a box with homemade biscuit and egg sandwiches. When she awoke at 8:00 the coffee was already made. That meant Tom had seen her asleep on the sofa. She wasn't sure if she was happy or sad he didn't wake her. For a moment she wondered what it would be like waking up next to him.

Wouldn't do anyone any good to go there, she decided. Her life was in Portland, Oregon not Broken Bow, Oklahoma. She had a career in music. She had the best of friends who had showed her what real family was like. She had a full life without Tom Pawlak and she would again after her father died.

For now, she needed to thank him for all he had done for her father. She also wanted to know why. The one and only time her father had stood up for her was when Tom Pawlak had treated her so terribly. He'd banned Tom from the property. So what changed in the last seven years? And what was in it for Tom?

She packed everything into a canvas bag and set it on the counter. She hurried down the hall and peeked into her father's room to see if he needed anything. He was still asleep. In fact, it appeared he hadn't moved at all since she left him yesterday. She moved stealthily toward the bed and lowered her ear near his mouth. She let out the breath she was holding. Yes, her father was still breathing, just deep in sleep.

The worry of him dying too fast speared her again as she turned back toward the kitchen. She could only handle one worry at a time. Right now she had to find Tom.

Sarah found Tom halfway down the vegetable field, planting seeds in the rain. He didn't even have on a slicker. His soaked shirt stuck to his skin, outlining every muscle as he worked. The normally tight curls of hair had lengthened and drooped over his forehead. Focused on the task, he moved quickly, pushing the walk-behind seeder down the row. After he finished the row, he turned to the next one.

Kip was laying the front porch, smartly staying out of the rain. He barked as she ran for cover.

When Tom glanced up, she waved and pointed to her bag. "Breakfast?" she yelled.

His eyes widened and he smiled. He held up an index finger to indicate he needed a little time, and then he worked his way down the next row getting closer with each planting. She watched his every movement—the way his arms flexed as he pushed the seeder in front of him; the way he walked a straight line. The way he bent to adjust the drill or reseat the wheels in the row. Her heart did a little skip as he got closer and closer.

"Breakfast? For me?" he asked as he climbed the porch steps and stood in front of her, water cascading off his body.

"Is there somewhere dry to enjoy this?" Sarah motioned toward the door. "Or at least chairs to pull onto the porch?"

"I don't really have a kitchen," Tom said. "I use the main house kitchen, and generally cook for Jack. Before he stopped eating." He held open the door for her and motioned her inside. "I do have a couple chairs though, if want to sit."

She nodded and stepped through the door. It was a studio apartment. A queen size bed took up most of the room. She couldn't ignore it. Along one wall his clothes hung on a pipe. A small dresser also served as a nightstand on one side of his bed. Next to that was a door that must be the bathroom.

She quickly turned away from the scene and noticed the small table right near the front door. She'd completely missed it when she'd stepped into the room. It was a very small bistro table with two chairs crowded into a corner. On the other side of the door was a small counter with a microwave and a cupboard below.

Sarah swallowed and set the canvass bag on the table, facing the front door. "I made biscuit and egg sandwiches," she said over her shoulder, making sure she did not look toward the bed again. She didn't even want to think about Tom's bed being so close. "And fresh hot coffee." She turned toward the cupboards beneath the sink and microwave. "Any chance you have coffee cups or shall we drink out of the thermos?"

Tom laughed behind her. "I'm not such a Neanderthal that I don't have any dishes." He brushed her back as he opened a cupboard below the microwave and withdrew two plates and two coffee cups.

She had to turn toward him to take the dishes. She held out her hands as she turned and then stopped. Her eyes immediately tracked to the bed again. Flustered, she felt her cheeks heat and quickly looked back to him. No that made it worse. Now she could picture him in the bed.

She swallowed. "I...uh." Her hands shaking, she took the plates from him. The cups rattled. "Thanks. I'll...uh...get things set up."

He cocked his head to one side and a small smile formed in one corner of his mouth. She recognized that smile from when they were together in high school. It said, I'm about to kiss you. She turned and quickly set the dishes on the table and busied herself pouring coffee, setting the plates. Next she would have to reheat the egg sandwiches and get them plated.

"I'm going to take a moment and change into dry clothes. Okay?" Tom said to her back.

She nodded. "It will be hot and ready when you come back."

He chuckled as his footsteps retreated toward the dresser. "That would be real nice," he said before she heard the bathroom door close.

Sarah slid into the chair facing the front door and held her face in her hands trying to stop her heart from beating double time. What was wrong with her? She knew what a bedroom looked like. Just because it was Tom's bedroom was no reason to go all fluttery. She couldn't possibly still have feelings for him. She hated him. Didn't she?

She took a deep breath and plated the egg sandwiches. She put the first plate in the small microwave and pressed the button that said reheat.

The only thing she could think is that because of all that was going on with her dad, she was extra emotional. Maybe she was also feeling a little thankful for all Tom had done too. But she certainly didn't have feelings for him. Not like she did before.

The microwave buzzed and she took the plate out and put the other plate in. After pushing the button again she forced herself to look directly at the bed again.

It's just a bed, like any other bed, she told herself. Of course it would be prominent in here because he had to build this little apartment himself. He didn't really need anything else.

She took a deep breath and let it out. Okay. I'm good. No problem here. No deep feelings. It's just a bed.

Tom emerged from the bathroom dry and shirtless. Sarah just stared and held her breath. She couldn't move.

He raised an eyebrow then bent to the dresser next to the bed and pulled out a black T-shirt and put it on. In bright orange letters it said Oklahoma State Football.

She focused on letting out her breath. "The … uh … it's ready. Everything is hot."

He took four big steps and was suddenly face-to-face with her. "Thanks, Sarah."

She didn't move. She couldn't. Every part of her body was straining toward his.

He looked straight at her and a half smile formed, but his eyes revealed sadness, a kind of resignation. His chest rose on a deep intake of breath and he gently touched her arm. "You didn't have to do this, but I appreciate it. Let's eat so I can get back to finish the seeding." Then he let go and stepped to one side, breaking the spell of warmth as the chair scratched on the floor when he pulled it away from the table.

Sarah lowered to her chair, still in a haze. She said nothing as she nibbled on the breakfast sandwich.

Tom took two big bites. "This is real good," he said. "Maybe you can take over some of the cooking now that you're here. Would that be okay with you?"

"Yes, of course," she said. "Please tell me all the things I can do to help. I didn't know you were working off the farm too. You must be exhausted."

"It's not so bad most of the time," he said. "I've gotten used to splitting my time. It started when I was going to college. Then, when I got my degree, I kept the second job because I needed money to fix things around here."

"College? Degree?" Sarah asked.

He pointed to his T-shirt. "About half online and the other half in actual classrooms. It took me six years, but I did it."

Sarah was pleasantly surprised. Tom had always been smart. When they were dating he had plans to become a veterinarian. But then Amanda came along, and all the other girls he toyed with, then it seemed it was more important to him to drink and party than anything else.

"Did you get started toward becoming a vet then?"

"No, I decided to get a general business degree. I wanted a degree I could use anywhere in the country. Also, the business major had the most online classes available which was important as I traveled a lot to keep jobs."

Tom poured another cup of coffee from his thermos. "Can I refill you?"

"No. I had a lot at the house before I came looking for you. You can have the rest, and my thermos too."

She took another bite of her sandwich and tried to reconcile the Tom she left with this new man sitting beside her.

"Girlfriend? Fiancée?" she asked, then thought better. "I'm sorry. None of my business."

He covered her hand with his. "No one, Sarah. No one for the last six years."

She couldn't catch her breath. Did she dare believe? No. It wasn't possible. Not someone who was seducing every girl in town. He couldn't possibly go six years without sex after all that.

"How about you?" He asked, his voice just above a whisper.

"No," she said softly.

"No, you won't tell me or no you don't have someone in your life."

"No, I don't have someone in my life. I've dated, but there's no one right now. I'm still waiting for the right man. The man I will marry."

Sarah broke away from his gaze and looked out the window. What was she doing? She absolutely was not going to hope. She couldn't. She couldn't face that hurt again.

Tom stood and pulled a slicker from the peg near the door. "I need to get back to seeding. Then I need to get your dad up and to the toilet and maybe a bath."

"I'll help," Sarah said, standing and getting her own raincoat.

"I...uh...don't think you want to do that, Sarah. He's pretty difficult to lift and I'm not sure you could handle everything. Besides he'd be pretty embarrassed."

"I meant I'll help with the seeding. With two of us it will go faster. There is a second one in the barn still, right? I can remember both

Mom and Dad pushing the walk-behinds and seeding together when I was young. I can take a different vegetable."

"Are you sure?"

She zipped up her jacket and pulled the drawstring of the hood to secure it. "Yes. And afterward, I need to learn how to care for my father. I need to understand what will happen. Maybe I can't lift him or carry him, but I suspect that…" Her voice caught in her throat as she contemplated his death once more. "I have to accept he is going to die soon, and I can help with his care."

Tom turned her toward him and lifted her chin. "Sarah, you don't have to do this. It's difficult enough watching him deteriorate without having to see everything that's going on with his body. I'm fine with doing it all. I already know what will happen."

She shook her head. "I *have* to do this. I *want* to do this for him. Don't you see? It's part of my penance for not paying attention, for not seeking him out or even wondering what was going on with him the last two years. I've asked him to forgive me, but how do I forgive myself, Tom? How do I… " She dropped her head so he wouldn't see the tears. She'd done so much crying since she arrived here that she imagined there would be no tears left.

Tom gathered her into his arms and she rested her cheek against his chest and held on to him. It felt good, even better than old times.

"I do understand, Sarah." He moved his palm in circles on her back. "We will get through this. We'll do this together. One day at a time."

CHAPTER 7

TOM PUSHED THE WALK-BEHIND SEEDER through the mud. The constant drizzle of rain made the ground slippery. He struggled to walk a straight line. He and Sarah walked in opposite directions in their rows. As they came toward the middle, he checked to make sure she was doing okay. She knew how to do the seeding. She'd probably been helping with it since she was old enough to push the thing. Strong and determined, she worked row after row in the slipper mud.

"Noooo," Sarah screamed.

Tom looked over and her seeder was on its side with her fighting to right it.

"I'm okay," she shouted toward him. "Go back to work, I'll get this thing right."

He wanted to run over and help, but he knew she wouldn't appreciate it. Instead he walked with his own seeder, taking surreptitious looks toward her. She tugged and pulled while slipping in the mud twice. Finally, it was upright and she was on her knees picking up the seeds that had spilled.

"We are walking straight," she said as they approached each other again in the middle. "I'm not letting a stupid seeder get the best of me."

Tom smiled and tipped his hat. One moment she was standing, the next she slipped in the mud and skidded on her stomach right into the seeder. Mud splashed up into her face and through her wet hair, but she didn't seem to care. Her laughter was carried away on the breeze.

When he approached, she had managed to stand. Then she dove toward the wet ground on purpose and just slid on her belly away from him. When she came to a stop, Sarah slapped both hands on the ground and splashed up a mixture of mud and water. She tried to move the hair out of her eyes, but in the process smeared the mud across her face.

She looked up at him. "I used to love playing in the mud. I would make the most amazing mud pies and Mom would pretend to eat them."

He offered her a hand up. When she stood he gingerly moved the bedraggled hair from her cheek and tucked it behind her ear. "Do you have any mud pies for me?" he asked

"This is all that's left." She smeared her hand across his face, and giggled. "Are we having fun yet?" she asked, her lips trembling. He wasn't sure if she was cold or about to cry.

Fun? No. Nothing about this was fun. But it wasn't the trial he expected either. He couldn't believe there was still a spark between them. In fact, the attraction was stronger than ever. Did he dare hope that the answer to his prayers for a marriage partner would be Sarah?

"We need to get moving," he said. "They say the rain will get worse later this evening. I'd like to get these in and everything covered before it hits."

She stared at him as if he were someone she'd never seen before. He cocked his head, trying to determine what it meant.

"If you need to go inside, I understand," he said. "I can finish this on my own."

"Oh, no. You aren't going to treat me like he little woman who needs to be safely ensconced by the fire at home," she responded, coming alive. "I'm going to do my half even if I fall down on every row." Then she took hold of the seeder and started walking again.

Tom shook his head in amazement. He'd spent the last six years trying to become the man Sarah had expected him to be. Not as much for her as for himself. He'd figured that wherever Sarah had gone she was married, with children, and happy.

He'd even tried to return to church. He ended up there a couple times a year. He found some special comfort in the sermons, even though he still wasn't sure if he really believed. There was just too much pain in his own life—in the world for that matter—that he still couldn't square with the concept of a loving God. Now, his life had come full circle. Sarah was back and she was yearning for him as much as he was for her—whether she admitted it or not.

Three more passes and they would be done. Three more passes and then the truly hard work would begin: helping Sarah to understand how her father would die.

On the last pass, he finished his row and pulled the seeder from the ground. He turned to take it back to the barn and wash it down when he saw Sarah slip and fall into the mud at the end of her last row. He waited a minute for her to get up on her own, but she wasn't moving. He released the seeder and ran in her direction.

"Sarah," he shouted as he ran.

He got to the end of the row and found her laying face up and laughing so hard that tears were rolling down her face. He bent over her and took a handkerchief from his pocket to wipe off the mud.

She looked at him, her hands squishing the mud at either side. She tried to stand again but the mud sucked at her feet and hands.

"It's just rain," she said, unmoving. "Just rain. Just mud. Just a father dying who I don't know how to forgive. Just a farm I don't know how to run. Just…"

He pulled her to a sitting position and sat in the mud with her. "It's okay," he said. "The rain will pass and the sun will come out again. This is a difficult time, but we can get through it."

"Can we?" she asked. "It feels like the rain is laughing at me, enjoying the never-ending downward spiral of my life."

She burst out with laughter again and tears leaked onto her cheeks. It was like she couldn't decide whether to laugh or cry. She couldn't stop herself from doing both.

He shook her. "Sarah. You're hysterical."

"I'm…not…hysterical," she managed between bursts of giggling.

Her little laugh became a bigger laugh. The tears stopped and the bubbling, gurgling, sound grew as she laughed louder and harder. In a setting of dripping, wet, muddy hair shone a red, blustery face.

"I just realized that God has a sense of humor, and he's blessed me with his grand joke." She burst into gut wrenching laughter again, then packed her hands with mud and smeared mud all over Tom's jacket.

Tom frowned, unsure of the turn from despondence to laughter. But her laughter became infectious.

"A joke?" he asked.

"You. Me. Life. Love. Death. It's all a muddy mess. Don't you see? I've been wallowing in the mud, when I should be playing in it.

She grabbed mud with both hands and slung it at him.

"So, you want to mud wrestle? Is that it?" He grabbed his own bit of mud and deftly painted a streak on each of the cheeks he had so carefully cleared with his handkerchief earlier.

They tussled a bit with him on top holding her down, and then she reversed him so that she was on top holding him down. Suddenly, she stopped fighting and just looked at him. Her eyes widened and she stared.

"What is it, Sarah? What's wrong."

"Everything's wrong," she said. Then she pulled his face to hers. "Because I don't want to play like children. I want this." She pressed her lips to his and kissed him with abandon. It was just as he remembered—delicate and hard mixed together, fragile innocence with sensuous assurance. He held her on top of him, and responded with his own kisses until they were both breathless.

SARAH LAID her head on his chest, both of them covered from head to toe with mud. She'd given up on hiding her feelings for him. She had poured all her hopes and dreams into that kiss, in the mud, in the driving rain. And she prayed this time Tom didn't run.

Yes, God definitely had a sense of humor to bring her to Tom again during the most confusing time of her life.

"Sarah, I—"

She put a finger to his lips. "No. Don't say anything. Don't make any promises. Don't ask any questions. Just be."

He kissed her again and she felt the love in that kiss, it was tender and sensual at the same time. It was filled with promises from the past and for the future. She could barely believe it, but she relished it just the same.

"I never stopped loving you," he said. "I never prayed for God to bring you back to me. I only prayed that you had found happiness and that God would help me do the same without you."

She wasn't sure what he was saying. Tom prayed? About her? Could this be true?

"I'm not sure what this is," she said. "I mean you. Me. Us. I don't understand what I'm feeling right now. I only know that it feels right. It makes no sense to me. I haven't forgiven you, yet I want you. It's…"

She heard the crunch of gravel and the sound of a heavy car coming up the driveway. She rolled away from Tom and he helped her stand, steadying her against his broad torso.

A luxury Land Rover parked next to the barn, beneath the overhang, very close to Tom's door. A slender foot in long spiky heels appeared first beside the car. Then a petite blonde stepped out in a body hugging, neon-blue sweater dress. The woman walked up to the porch and knocked.

Kip darted off the porch and barked as he ran toward the woman. He stopped about three feet away and growled.

"I've never known Kip to growl," Sarah said. "It appears you have an interesting visitor."

Tom whistled for Kip. He looked at Tom and then back at the woman as if undecided.

Sarah slapped her thigh. "Come, Kip. Come."

The dog ran back and stood beside her, but his tail was not wagging.

"Who is it?" Sarah asked.

"You don't want to know."

"Why don't I want to know?"

"It's Amanda."

He held tight to her waist when she tried to step away. "It's not what you think."

Sarah looked to the sky and held up her fist. "Not funny anymore. I'm not Job. Do you hear me?"

Tom chuckled. "Maybe I should call you Saint Sarah."

Sarah faced him. Her hand fisting his shirt. "Tell me why she's here. The truth."

"She's married with two kids. Has been for a decade, but she sleeps with anyone with money who will have her. Her husband is a good guy. I don't know why she sleeps around."

"And?"

He let out a breath. "And…she wants to add me to her man harem."

"I see."

Tom uncurled her fingers from his shirt. "No, you don't see. I don't want her. I never wanted her. Even in high school. After that one weekend, I never slept with her again."

"Then why does she keep coming around?"

He shrugged. "I don't know. I tell her the same thing every time. Maybe it's because I'm one of the few to say no to her." He took both her hands and squeezed. "Come on, let's face the music together. Maybe seeing you here will finally make her leave me alone."

Maybe siccing the dog on her would be even better, Sarah thought to herself. Not a very Christian thought, she admitted. Maybe just let the dog scare her a little, she amended.

In high school, Amanda had always hung with the rich, mean girl clique. It wasn't that she picked on Sarah. Amanda didn't think Sarah was worth thinking about. But after that horrible weekend, Amanda went out of her way to make sure Sarah knew that she'd had sex with Tom and went into details about all the different ways they'd done it.

She told Sarah that because Tom had needs Sarah refused to meet that he was now working his way through all her girlfriends. Amanda would stop by Sarah's work and let her know who Tom was with that week and what special sexual favor another girl did for him that Sarah would never do. It was as if it was all Sarah's fault that Tom was forced to bed every girl in town just to learn how it's done.

Though she'd questioned that logic at first, Sarah now knew better than that. None of it was her fault. There is nothing wrong with wanting to remain a virgin until she married. In fact, she was glad she hadn't been just another girl in Tom's journey toward sexual knowledge.

Sarah bent and picked up another clump of mud and rubbed it all over Tom's face again. She made sure it was caked on pretty thick this time.

She grinned. "Okay, Don Juan, let's see if she wants you now. I'll bet she won't kiss this face. It's time for me to be the one in control."

He put a strong hand below her knees and lifted her into his arms and she gasped. "I am under your control," he said, walking like a zombie might. He laughed long and hard as he carried her all the way back to the porch with Kip trailing behind.

"What in the world happened to you?" Amanda asked staring at them as he approached.

He put Sarah down, but drew her protectively into his side once more. He used the sleeve of his shirt to rub away the dirt from his mouth.

"Hi Amanda. Long time no see." Sarah said. "Remember me?"

Amanda looked only at Tom. "I don't know who this is or what sick game you're playing, but I'll wait until you've showered to talk to you."

"I've already showered today," Tom said and Sarah laughed.

"Mud wrestling with a hooker? Tom, are you really so desperate for sex. You know I'd be happy to…anytime."

"A hooker?" Sarah asked, looking up at him. "A virgin hooker, how unique." She pulled Tom's muddy face to hers. "Did I hook you?"

Tom smiled. "I've been hooked on you forever." Then he planted a long kiss on her lips.

Amanda stomped her foot. "This is not funny. It's disgusting. Look at you. What's going on, Tom? What does this skank have on me?"

Tom straightened. "I forgot the introductions. Amanda Davidson meet Sarah Cosgrave. Sarah, Amanda."

Amanda's jaw dropped. "No. Not Sarah. It couldn't be."

"Yes, I'm still Sarah." Sarah smiled and held out her muddy hand as if to shake. Amanda recoiled and took a step back. "You used to be Amanda Cooper, right? We were always seated near each other in elementary school. Not that we ever talked."

"Well, I…"

"Tom tells me you're married now with two kids," Sarah continued. "How wonderful for you."

"I…Sarah…I can't believe…I thought you were…" Amanda sputtered.

"A hooker," Sarah supplied. "Or was it a looker? I'm not sure I heard exactly what you said."

"What is it you wanted?" Tom again put his arm around Sarah's waist and pulled her close. "As you can see we are a little busy now. So, unless it's an emergency…"

"I just wanted to talk, to catch up. But I can see this isn't a good time. I'll come back later tonight, when you are more… presentable."

"The answer is the same as it's always been, Amanda. You need to work out whatever your problems are with your husband. I'm not available. I haven't ever been available to you since that one mistaken weekend."

"That wasn't a mistake," Amanda said. "I know I didn't treat you right, but I was young. Naïve. I didn't know what I was doing."

"Naïve is the last thing you were," Tom said.

"It was my mistake to end it. I just want to see if we can get the old spark back." The invitation in her voice was palpable.

"No. We can't," Tom said. "Now go home."

Amanda shook her finger at him. "You owe me, Tom. I did set you up well with all my friends." She looked directly at Sarah. "You do know he screwed everyone but you, right? Even if he's screwing you now, it doesn't really count. I mean it's a pity screw. What with your father dying and all."

"That is completely out of line," Tom said. "Leave now or I'll call the sheriff to arrest you for trespassing."

Amanda's eyes widened. "I can't believe you are screwing her and not me." She scanned Sarah as if assessing what he saw in her. Then she huffed and tapped her foot, dismissing her.

"Well, I can wait for you. I've done it before and I'll do it again." She turned to Sarah. "You do know that after you left I had to stay with him, screw him every day, help him get over you."

"That's not true," Tom said.

"Of course, you would say that." She waved her hand at Tom, rejecting his statement. "You know some men have a thing for virgins. I'm afraid that's all it is with you and Tom now. Because he knows what good sex is like. He's had everything and more from me and my friends. You could never satisfy him, no matter how much you try. There are some things he likes, truly dark and wonderfully twisted things you would never do for him. No matter what he'll need those things and you'll eventually lose him."

"None of that is true. She satisfies me just the way she is," Tom said.

Amanda ignored him. "Really it all comes down to power in the end. Just because he could never have you, he's held on to this unrealistic fantasy. This fantasy of breaking you in, being the first."

"Leave. Now." Tom pointed toward her car.

"Did it hurt when he did you?" Amanda touched Sarah's hand, but Sarah withdrew. "Oh, I see it did. He's never had a virgin before, you know. Most men know that the first time with a virgin is awful. All that pain, all that yelling, and the bleeding. Just messy. I'm sure you don't want to do it again."

Sarah couldn't find words, but she also didn't believe what Amanda was saying. For the most part. Perhaps some of it was true, but Tom had said he'd never slept with her after Sarah left or any of Amanda's friends.

"Tom can be such a brute," Amanda continued. "He can't help it. I happen to like it hard, but you, your delicate, your—

"We haven't had sex," Sarah yelled, a little too loudly. She wanted to put a stop to this. Maybe if she told the truth Amanda would go away.

"Ohhhhh." Amanda touched her index finger to her lips and smiled. "Oh, now I see. Good for you, Sarah. Good for you sticking to your beliefs."

"Now go," Sarah said. "Tom doesn't want you here and I don't want you here. There is no reason to stay. There is no reason to come back.

"I'll leave, don't worry." Then she looked at Tom and smiled. "She's not really staying is she? I mean she lives somewhere else right?"

Sarah stepped in front of Tom and moved within six inches of Sarah's smiling face. "I don't know how long I'm staying. I don't know what will happen after my father dies. I may have to stay on for years to run the ranch. In fact, Tom and I may have to get married immediately after the funeral so that we can start making little babies right away to get enough help to make the farm viable for me."

Amanda's mouth formed I little O and her eyes darted to Tom and then back to her. She backed toward her car. "I can see this isn't a good time." She opened the door and slid into the seat, her tight skirt hiking up her thigh.

Sarah waved. "Good to see you, Amanda."

Amanda narrowed her eyes and slammed the door shut, then took off back down the dirt road, spewing rocks and mud behind her.

Tom hugged Sarah, picking her up and twirling in a circle. "You were amazing. You stood right up to her."

Sarah giggled. "I was wasn't I? It felt so good to not be afraid of her, to not care what she thought of me. I wasn't too mean was I? Is it bad of me for telling a little lie and feeling so good about it?"

"No, you deserve to feel good."

She smiled, but then it turned tentative. How much of what Amanda said was true? She figured most of it wasn't, but many lies have truth hidden in them."

"I've never heard her be so mean before. Was she like this to you all the time, when you lived here?"

She nodded. "After you and she…and all her friends…the year before I left she made it a point to tell me everything that was happening in every detail."

He tentatively reached for her hand. "I'm sorry. I'm sorry I put you through that."

"And what she said about after I left?"

"All lies. After you left is when I left too. I couldn't stand that I hurt you so much. I couldn't stand myself."

"And when you came back? Did you hook up again? Ever?"

"No." He pulled her up the stairs onto the porch and into his place. He wet a cloth at the sink and gently wiped her face clean. Then he took the mud off his own face. He stripped off his muddy shirt and held his arms wide, inviting Sarah back into his embrace.

She hesitated. Deep down she believed Tom. But she couldn't help but question it again when Amanda went on and on in graphic detail. Why would she do that if it wasn't at all true?

Tom dropped his arms. "I can't prove it to you. I can't prove that she's lying, because it's her word against mine. I don't know her agenda. I don't know what she thinks she'll gain by her lies, because there is no way I would ever consider being with her. After today, there is no way I would even give her a minute more of my time."

"I believe you," Sarah said. "It's just hard to have her bring it all up again, to have her control my emotions again with her lies. I thought I'd put it behind me. I thought I had more strength now. But when she kept going on and on, I questioned what I was doing."

She moved into Tom's arms and held tight around his waist. There was too much going on in her life right now to let Amanda get in the middle of it.

He enveloped her and breathed a heavy sigh. "All I can say is that I love you. In these past weeks, I hope you've seen my true character. I am not the scared, angry boy I was in high school. I will never lie to you, Sarah."

"We both deserve to feel good," She said and raised her lips to his.

He dipped his head and gently explored her lips. "I love you," he whispered between kisses. "I'll never let you go again."

She pressed into him and opened for his tongue. She wanted to feel him all around her. She wanted his touch, his kiss, his very breath to reassure her of his love. She engaged in the dance of tongues. She thrilled to the touch of his hands on her cheeks, on her neck. She arched toward him wanting more.

He groaned. "My sweet Sarah." He drew her toward the bathroom, kissing her as he danced her backward. "Let's wash the mud off us. Join me? The shower is small but we can make it work."

She wanted to. She could barely catch her breath as he plundered her mouth once more. She wanted so much more. If they made love, she would know for sure his feelings.

He backed her against the shower door and quickly drew his T-shirt over his head, then pulled her into his bare chest and held her head tight against him. She good feel his accelerated heart beat. Her breath panted like his as she contemplated what to do next.

He stepped back only an inch as he reached for her T-shirt and took the hem with both hands.

She put her hand over his and concentrated on slowing her breathing, her wild thoughts, all that she wanted right this minute.

"Sarah?"

With effort she pushed against his chest and he took a step back. "I'll admit, there is nothing I would like to do more than be with you right now, to understand what it is like to love someone physically as well as spiritually. But ... you know I can't."

"Why not? I love you. You love me. Let's start where we left off. Where I messed up."

"Why do you think I've been saving myself all these years for the right man?"

"Yes, for me." Tom bent to kiss her again but she wriggled away.

"For marriage," Sarah said. "You know I don't believe in sex before marriage."

Tom's brow furrowed. "I guess I knew that was what you believed in high school, but that night—the night I didn't show up—I thought you were—"

Sarah pressed two fingers to his lips. "I was. But it didn't happen and now I know I want to wait. I want it to be special. I want it to be with the person I know I will spend the rest of my life with."

"But your twenty-six years old. No one waits at our age."

"I do," she said softly.

He was stunned. He respected her beliefs, but after all these years and having her here, in front of him, knowing she loved him again, he didn't want to wait.

He sighed. Instant gratification was the past Tom. Karma was biting him in the butt, again.

He kissed her again. This time a light, accepting brush of the lips. "The day we get married will be the happiest day of my life. I will wait for you, Sarah Cosgrave."

"Is that a proposal?"

"It's a promise," he said. "The proposal will come after I talk to your father and you know all my faults."

"I already know about your promiscuous past. If I didn't, Amanda just reminded me in spades."

"And if you don't leave within the next minute, you'll learn about my current secret," he said.

"What's that?"

"That I only have so much patience before I will haul you into the shower with me, clothed or not."

"Oh!" She backed out of the bathroom then hurried toward the front door. "I, uh, better leave then."

He captured her hand and she turned. He kissed her again and again as he backed her toward the front door. When they reached it he trapped her between his body and the closed door. This time he kissed her with all the passion he was fighting to hold at bay. When he thought he would surely explode, he pulled her to one side, turned the knob, and opened the door. His breaths were deep as he held her tight against him again. "This is your last chance for that hot shower."

Her eyes widened and she backed over the threshold. "I'm…going."

She smiled, kissed him on the cheek, then turned and fled down the stairs.

He watched her long hair flicking bits of mud behind her as she ran to the main house with her arms wide in happy surprise. Just before she reached the house, she twirled back toward him and waved.

Then she dropped her muddy shoes on the porch, turned and disappeared inside the door. Tom shook his head in amazement. Sarah was back and she still loved him. And when she loved, her passion was palpable. She didn't kiss like a virgin and he'd bet that, when they finally married, he'd be the lucky receiver of passion beyond his wildest dreams.

He closed the door. He really needed that shower, and he was considering making it very cold.

Sarah wrapped her arms around herself and hugged the day to her. She still couldn't believe that mud could be so much fun. If her friends could see her now they would be shocked. Well, all except Rachel. She would say something like, "About time. When did the clothes come off?" Then give her that I-can't-believe-you-didn't-jump-in-the-shower-with-him look. Oh she wanted to, she wanted to find out what happened beyond kisses.

What a wonderful day! Who knew that mud could make her sexy? That shy, conservative Sarah Cosgrave would be kissed so passionately that she could barely think, or that she would best her nemesis, the beautiful and rich Amanda Davidson, while covered with mud.

She laughed again as she recalled Amanda's dismay at learning that Sarah and Tom were back together. Sarah stepped out of her clothes, leaving them in a pile near the door. As she stepped under the spray she watched the magical mud swirl down the drain, and with it doubt crept back in.

Why would Amanda continue to come to visit Tom after all this time, come with an open invitation for an affair? Tom said he'd never accepted her advances but she came anyway. Could that really be true? No woman would keep coming if she knew it was certain nothing would ever happen. What wasn't he telling her? Had Sarah been too quick to believe his explanation?

She shampooed her hair with a vengeance and scrubbed all the rest of the dirt from her arms and face. The water cooled and she turned it off quickly and stepped out of the shower. She shivered in the cold realization that perhaps she'd been a fool. Perhaps she saw in Tom's actions only what she wanted to see. Perhaps it was all leading to get her in bed, not to a relationship and the forever marriage she dreamed of. She wrapped a towel around herself and picked up the dirty clothes, chucking them in the hamper near the laundry.

She hurried to her room to change. Better to wake up now and be cautious of Tom's motives than to imagine feelings that might not exist. Sure he said he still loved her and wanted to marry her, but that was in a moment of happy abandonment. Could she really trust that? Or was he just in lust?

She flopped onto her bed in comfy sweats and a long-sleeved shirt. Things were moving too fast. She'd barely been here two days and things were more confusing than ever.

Sarah grabbed her phone and dialed Theresa's number. Theresa was like a mother to her—actually the mother of the entire band. She'd been married and divorced and raised Kat on her own. If anyone knew the truth about men and love it would be Theresa.

When Theresa answered Sarah cried with relief, then she let it all out at once. Her father's condition, the realization that she was still in love with Tom, all that had happened today that seemed so wonderful, and finished with Amanda and all her renewed doubts. Finally, she stopped talking and waited.

"Whew. That's a load," Theresa said after a long pause. "So many emotions, so much to take in."

"Yeah, I know. That's why I called. I don't know what to think. I don't know what to do. Should I act like I'm still in love with him? Should I believe him? Should I trust him?"

"Well…you make it sound like everything is yes or no. Perhaps you should consider a maybe in there too."

"Maybe what? Maybe I love him? Maybe he loves me? Maybe he screws around with Amanda and lied to me? Again."

"Whoa. Slow down there. Take some breaths."

Sarah closed her eyes and breathed.

"Maybe," Theresa started drawing out the word. "Maybe you need to not make any decisions about anything yet. Maybe you need to slow down and see what develops over the next several weeks."

"But I want to know now. I don't want to be in love with him again and just get hurt. I don't think I could live through it a second time. If it's not going to happen, I want to stop all these feelings now."

"Honey, the fact is you are in love with him. You can't just turn it off. I suspect you never stopped loving him. Why do you think you never dated a guy more than two months? Because they never compared to your memory of the good Tom. Now, here you are face-to-face with the good Tom of your dreams. Just accept it. You are in love with him."

"But I don't want to be."

"That's not true. You do want to be madly in love. And you want him to be madly in love with you. What you don't want is to be hurt again."

Sarah had nothing to say to that. It seemed so much easier just to hate Tom and protect herself than to be open to him, to trust.

"Honey, there is no way to live life without being hurt. It happens even when someone loves you very much. Even if you're married with loving children, you will still be hurt. Something always happens to cause hurt."

"That doesn't sound right," Sarah said. "How can two people who love each other hurt each other? I thought love conquered all."

"Now you're sounding like Kat. You know life isn't like a romance movie. Things happen that challenge your belief in yourself, your partner, even your children. It's what you do with those challenges that make or break a relationship."

"And this is one of those challenges?" Sarah asked.

"Yes. You are both dealing with two big challenges at the same time: your dying father and your renewed relationship. Both have powerful emotions of love and loss and regret. Just one of those would be enough to make life confusing and difficult to navigate. I suggest you deal with the immediate one first, your father, and don't make any decisions about Tom. How the two of you work together to care for your father will show you a lot about who Tom is now and who you are now."

"So, don't pursue anything romantic now?"

"Do what your heart dictates, Sarah. Trust yourself and what you see in Tom."

"But my heart isn't wise," Sarah said. "It's in love, it wants to believe him. It wants everything to work out. It wants to shut out any distrust. And that might be the stupidest thing ever, because it means the hurt will be so much worse."

Theresa sighed. "I don't know what else to say to help you. I wish I could be there with you. I wish we all could be there to help you through this. But you are going to have to take each day as it comes. Try to just be present with whatever is happening that day. Don't think of the past and don't think of the future. Just think of what you need to do that day. Honey, it's only going to get harder."

"I know," Sarah whispered. "And that scares me even more."

"You know I'm only a phone call away."

"Yes. Thanks. Give my love to everyone in the band."

"I will."

Sarah hung up and hugged her knees to her chest. She sat, unmoving for several minutes trying to take it all in, trying to just accept. But she couldn't help but let all the what-ifs in too. Then she put her head down and prayed.

It's just you and me, Lord. And I'm not too reliable right now. I'm open to any answers, in case you want to write them in the sky or something. Absent that, please help me to be patient. To take one day at a time. I'll try to listen for you. I really will. But right now I'm having trouble hearing. So, keep ringing me. Okay? Eventually, I'll pick up.

CHAPTER 8

TOM WAITED IN THE KITCHEN for Sarah to come for breakfast. He'd already scrambled eggs and cooked bacon. The coffee had been on for over an hour. He didn't remember sleeping much last night, even though he hadn't gone into work.

At 6:30 she walked in, still half asleep.

"Oh. I didn't expect to see you here. I thought you'd be back in the field or still asleep."

"What kind of toast would you like," he asked. "White or wheat?"

"You made breakfast?" Her voice sounded wary.

"I've been making breakfast for Jack and me for two years. That is when he used to eat it."

"Oh." She wrinkled her forehead. "Something wrong? You seem … I don't know … anxious."

"Let's eat first. White or wheat?"

She walked over to the pan of eggs and inhaled. "Yum. Cheese and onions too." She dished out a spoonful and took two pieces of bacon from the plate. Then she poured a mug of coffee. "I'll skip the bread. Thanks."

Tom nodded and filled his own plate with plenty of eggs and bacon, and two slices of wheat bread. He needed fortification. He was on his fifth cup of coffee. The old Tom would have been thinking of a drink right now, but not anymore. He wanted to be alert and fully in control of his faculties when he told Sarah about Jack. He had no idea how she would react, but he wanted to be ready for anything.

Sarah took a couple bites of eggs and a long gulp of coffee, and then she put her fork down and looked right at him. "I'm not going to wait until the end of breakfast to hear what you have to say. I'll just make all kinds of stuff up in my mind that would probably be a lot worse. So spill."

He shifted in his seat. "Last night I called my boss to tell him I'm taking a three-week leave now."

She lifted a fist to her mouth and he heard the intake of breath.

"When I checked on Jack last night he was a lot worse."

"No." Her eyes misted. "How bad?"

Tom twined his fingers through hers. "I'd hoped to have a few days to explain to you what the end would be like, but it looks like we will have to deal with it now."

"What? Are we talking days or hours?" Her voice shook with the question.

"I'm not sure. It all depends on if he's going to fight at all."

She turned her head away. "He won't fight." She swallowed. "He stopped fighting before I got here."

He watched her sit up straighter, clench her teeth and look him straight in the eyes, just like a soldier readying for battle. "Tell me what to expect. Tell me what I can do."

He'd expected her to cry, or at least shake and fall apart a bit. He didn't expect this strength.

"Do you want to know the physical things or what?"

"Everything. I want to know everything."

Tom nodded. "When I checked on him yesterday to bathe him, after we came in from the field, I noticed his stomach was distended. That means his liver has stopped functioning and he's retaining fluids. He's had it drained before, but this is even worse. It's the first sign of the end. Every breath rattled, which means he is not clearing secretions."

"Is he conscious at all?" she asked. If I talk to him will he know I'm there?"

"He's in and out of consciousness. Mostly out."

Sarah stood and paced. "What can we do? Should we take him to the hospital? Have them drain the fluid? Clear his lungs? What?"

Tom stood too and reached for her, but she shook her head and backed away.

"He doesn't want to go to the hospital. He has specific orders not to do any life-saving heroics."

"But what about what I want?" Sarah's voice raised with angry tears. "I'm not ready. I haven't forgiven him yet. Just this once, why can't he do what *I* want?"

"I'm sorry, Sarah. Even if he said yes, it would only buy him a few days extra. And we can't be sure of that. Do you want him to go through that excruciating pain for just a few more days? He might even die in the hospital. He would really hate that."

She crossed to the window over the sink and looked outside. Her shoulders were perfectly straight, her hands fisted. She was fighting for control. He knew it was hard. He'd gone through it with his mom. He'd been living with Jack's deterioration for two years. He'd done his grieving long ago. But for Sarah it was all new.

"It's so unfair," she said to the window, her voice quiet. "Just when I figure out how to forgive him I don't have a chance to make it right. To explain. To have a relationship with him again. I have so many questions to ask, so many things to understand."

"There may still be time," he said.

"Can I see him now? Is he conscious?"

"You can definitely see him. You can see him anytime you want. You don't need permission from me."

"What if he ... dies ... while I'm there?" She turned and looked at him, her face contorted with grief held at bay. "What do I do? Do I call you? Do I call the hospital?"

Tom gently took her hand. "You say goodbye in the best way you know how."

He walked with her to the other side of the house, to her father's room. "Do you want me to come in with you."

She stared at the door for several minutes.

"Just talk to him," Tom said. "Talk to him, even if he seems to be asleep. He may moan from time to time, but it doesn't mean he's in pain. So don't worry. He may not be able to respond, or even open his eyes, but I believe he can hear you."

She nodded and opened the door slowly. "Where will you be?"

"Wherever you want me to be."

"Will you wait in the kitchen? Or the living room? If I call will you come? Immediately?"

"Of course."

She faced the door, took a deep breath and walked in closing it behind her.

Tom waited a moment, just in case she needed him already. When he heard nothing he offered up a prayer, the first one he'd uttered since his mother's death.

Lord, as you know, we aren't exactly on speaking terms. Truth is I'm not even sure you exist. But here I am talking to you anyway. What matters is that Sarah believes in you, and she needs you right now. She is a good woman, Lord. A good woman who has carried a heavy burden for nearly twenty years. Please be with her and Jack. Help them both to let go and to part in peace.

He looked again toward the closed door. He swallowed several times to hold back the tears gathering in his throat. Tears for Sarah, for Jack, for his mother, for all the transgressions of his own past. He really hoped that God did exist and heard his prayer, because he knew there was nothing more he could do on his own.

SARAH SAT on the edge of the hospital bed in her father's bedroom, just as she had when she first arrived. Only this time he didn't open his eyes. He gave no indication he knew she was there.

She gently took his hand in hers and he moaned.

"Daddy? Do you need something? Water? Pain medication? What can I do?"

No response.

She rubbed circles on the back of his hand and waited. She remembered Tom said a moan didn't necessarily mean anything, but it sounded like it did. She just didn't know what. She waited for some sign that he knew she was there.

Nothing.

She raised his hand and brushed it with a kiss.

"I know I haven't been good lately about staying in touch. I just didn't know what to say, what to do. It seemed you didn't need me or want me."

She looked to see if anything had changed.

Nothing. She took another deep breath.

"I guess I should be grateful I can just talk without interruption. But it feels weird. I'm missing your opinions, even when you disagree with me. I'm missing your—" She gulped back tears. "I miss the big hug that greeted me just a couple days ago." She looked at him to see if she could gauge if he was hearing her at all. She let the tears flow freely. "I'm sorry, Daddy. I didn't know you were so sick."

It seemed crazy to ramble on, especially about her deepest feelings if he really wasn't there. She laid her head on his chest, just like she did when she was a little girl—before her mom died.

"I wanted to ask about Mom. I was so young when she died. I hardly remember her and I don't want to forget her. I hoped you could share pictures with me, memories … maybe even memories of before I was born. I want to know what she was like as an adult, what your relationship was like. I want to know if I'm anything like her. I want to know … if you really loved her."

Sarah felt the tears slipping onto the pajama top. She sat up again and wiped at her eyes. She didn't want to cry in front of her father, but once again it seemed she wouldn't get what she wanted.

"Then there's Tom. I'd like to know what happened that you let him back in your life. I'm glad you did, because he has been here for you when I wasn't. But I want to understand what you see in him. I want to know from you if I should trust him.

"I don't know what he's told you about his feelings. He says he loves me, but I don't know if that's true. He said it before and...well... you know what happened.

"The silly thing is I still love him, whether he loves me or not. It even sounds stupid hearing me say it. I know it's hard to believe after all these years and what he did to me, but I still love him. And the worst part is I love him even more than I did before. Isn't that crazy?"

She ran her hand across her father's forehead, brushing back what little hair he had. His skin felt clammy, like he'd just broken a fever. She stared at him for a long time then took his hand in hers again.

"Daddy, I don't have many examples of how love really works. I don't remember you and Mom together very much. I have friends in Portland who are madly in love with their husbands, but it's all still new to them. I want to know how love works for a marriage to last forever.

"With Tom, it seems I love him in spite of what he did. I don't like what he did. It was wrong and there is nothing he can do to make up for it. And there is something inside me that doesn't trust him because of that. But I think he's a new man now. And this man is amazing, Daddy. He's a combination of the Tom I knew before he went crazy, and a mature better Tom. But will this better Tom eventually leave? I can't be married to someone like that. I...I think if he left me again...I wouldn't recover.

"What do you see in him, Daddy? Do you see the old Tom or the new one? I wish you could talk, I wish you could tell me whether our marriage would work, whether we would stay together, whether I'll always be in love with him."

Sarah sighed. No response at all, not even a movement of an eyelid or any of his fingers resting in her hand.

"Please, Daddy. I need you now. Give me a sign if I should marry Tom Pawlak. Blink. Squeeze my hand. Do something. Even though you haven't been the best father, somehow I trust your opinion. I know you wouldn't lie to me about Tom. You never beat around the bush with your opinions about someone's character."

She waited again. There was no sign he was even alive except for his rattling, shallow breathing and the rise and fall of his chest. She had to accept he wasn't going to wake up. He wasn't going to give her any sign of understanding. It really was too late for them to talk. Too late to make amends.

She leaned her head onto his chest and listened for his heart beat. She could barely hear it. It was as if she could feel the life leaking out of him with each breath. The tears flowed freely now.

"Daddy, I forgive you," she said. "I want you to know that I accept you for who you are. I just wish..." a sob broke loose and she choked it back. "I just wish...we had another chance, so I could...so I could tell you I love you. I'm sorry I didn't tell you before. I love you so much."

She couldn't talk any more, she was crying so hard that words could no longer form. Her tears soaked her father's shirt through.

When her sobbing stopped, she felt something heavy on her head.

His hand rested on her head.

Then it slipped off. He was gone.

CHAPTER 9

SARAH SAT WITH TOM IN THE FRONT PEW. Just behind her were Theresa, Kat, Rachel and Michele. They'd all immediately arranged tickets and flew out to be with her. The basic wooden casket had a large bouquet draped over it, thanks to her Sweetwater Canyon family.

The church had a contemporary music trio with guitar, bass, and keyboards that opened the service with *Broken* by Lifehouse. She'd chosen that song because it reflected both her past with her father and her present. She couldn't help but sing the lyrics in her head. She said the words silently under her breath and let the tears come.

She closed her eyes and tried to forget all that had happened in the past week. The visit to the funeral home. The selection of a casket. All the questions they kept asking. The only thing she knew for sure was that she wanted the service to be at the church where she grew up and for her father to be buried next to her mother. But making those arrangements hadn't been easy.

She didn't know the new pastor of the church. As her father never went to church this pastor didn't know anything about him or Sarah, or any of their past. And her father, in his usual fashion, had never made any advance arrangements for his burial, and the plots near her mother's grave were all taken long ago. Tom helped her through that too. They finally decided that her father could be buried with her mother in the same plot.

The voices of the trio enveloped her on the chorus. The song reflected all of her feelings of overwhelming grief—not being able to breathe, the pain of not knowing the future or truly understanding the past. She had to trust in the Lord and simply hold on. Over the past week she had come to believe that living with the questions was as important as finding the answers. She realized that she needed to stop looking for answers from other people. She needed to look into her own heart and decide how to feel and what to do. No one else could do that for her. In doing that, and trusting in her own prayer and discernment, she would be embraced by God's healing love.

No one from the community had come to the service. She'd put an announcement in the small local paper in case there was someone who knew her father. Evidently her father had alienated everyone, especially his immediate neighbors. Michele squeezed her hand and Sarah held tight as the pastor read from scripture and offered the first prayer.

The service was interspersed with memories that Sarah and Tom had written of her father, and she cried silently through those readings. Then more scripture and words of healing followed. Sarah didn't select any hymns as she doubted there would be anyone to sing them.

The service ended with *Let Your Mercy Rain* by Chris Tomlin. She held the words close to her heart, asking for His mercy as they ended the song. She needed a healing rain.

AFTER THE BURIAL, the Sweetwater Canyon entourage went ahead to the house as Tom and Sarah thanked the funeral director, the pastor and the few additional church attendees. Finally, everyone was gone.

Tom stood quietly next to Sarah as she stared at the casket still raised over the open plot.

"When do they lower it?" she asked. "I remember when Mom died that they lowered it during the service and I was screaming at them to stop. I couldn't stand the thought of her being under all that dirt."

Tom put his arm around her shoulder. "You were only eight. You didn't fully understand."

"I don't fully understand now either." She stared again at the casket. "I'm glad they didn't do it during the service. I think that would be … too much."

Tom nodded. "When my mother died, she was cremated. I couldn't get it out of my mind that there would be no body for me to visit. That bothered me for a long time until I finally realized that it didn't matter if she had a grave to visit or was scattered in the river. I had to accept she was gone."

"Do you visit the river and talk to her?" Sarah asked, looking up to him.

"Yes." He looked across the breadth of the cemetery. "I know that some people find solace in visiting a grave, but I find my mother when I visit the river. The river is alive. It flows no matter the weather, and when I go there I feel her spirit there too."

"I don't feel Dad's spirit here," Sarah said, her voice raspy. "I don't feel him anywhere."

Tom drew her in front of him and held her shoulders. "You will. You've been apart for so long that he wasn't a part of your daily rhythm. Give it time. A lot has happened in the past couple of weeks."

He hugged her tight. "If you want to, Sarah, you will find a way to connect. Though he showed a lot of bravado about ending up in hell, he had an affinity for the land and for animals. I think, for him, that God was in nature—though I'm not sure he could have ever acknowledged that."

A tear stained face looked up at him. "You knew him so much better than I did. I wish I could have really known him."

"I'll share my memories with you. You don't have to do this alone."

She turned in his arms and looked at the casket one more time and then turned away. "Let's go. Let's go home."

KAT WAVED from the front porch of the house, then ran to the car and opened the passenger door. "You won't believe how much food Mom ordered. You won't have to cook for weeks, and it looks really yummy."

"Have you sampled any yet?" Sarah asked.

"Um…I was supposed to wait for you, so just a tiny sample of one of the finger sandwiches."

"And?"

"De-li-cious!"

Sarah laughed. It felt really good to laugh again.

Tom appeared at her side and took her hand. "I think we better get in there before it's all gone then."

Kat ran ahead and held open the door and bowed deeply. "Your food awaits madam."

Sarah stepped over the threshold and everyone greeted her at once —hugs, whispers of condolence, and more hugs. Lots and lots of hugs.

Theresa guided her inside to the couch and sat next to her. Kip arranged himself at her feet. Since her father died and through all the preparations, he had somehow known she needed him. He slept at the foot of the bed every night. Greeted her every morning. Whenever she'd been sad or confused, Kip would simply sidle up to her until she calmed.

A long table, arrayed with food, had been placed along the wall beneath the picture window. People were seated all over the living room. Rachel sat on Noel's lap, snugged into the single recliner in the room. Michele and David had claimed the settee, and Rachel's daughter, Claire, played quietly with Michele's toddler in the center of the living room.

Sarah watched Tom at the table as he placed small bites of food on a plate for her. Could she picture him as a permanent part of the Sweetwater Canyon family? She wanted to. She wanted to picture both of them with children of their own, getting together in family gatherings, all of their children playing together. But could he move to Portland? Or would he want to stay in Broken Bow? They hadn't even talked yet about the house and the farm and all that went with it.

Tom turned and walked toward her, balancing the plate in one hand and a glass of water in the other. He bent and brushed a kiss across her forehead before handing over the food. "Quite the extended family."

"Yes, I don't know what I'd do without them," Sarah said. "We've been through a lot together."

"Tom." Theresa moved to the other end of the couch and patted the middle seat. "Get yourself a plate and come sit down."

After everyone was seated with plenty of food, Theresa clapped her hands for attention. "We all know that we are here for Sarah and her father." She looked at Sarah. "But that doesn't mean we have to be maudlin the whole time. I'm betting that Sarah has had plenty of time of tears."

"I don't think I have any left," Sarah said, wondering what new bit of therapy Theresa had in mind now.

"When I was growing up and someone died, my family held a wake," Theresa continued. "It wasn't the everyone-stand-around-and-cry-for-three-days kind of wake. Instead, it was the tell stories kind of wake—embarrassing stories, funny stories, touching stories, whatever you like. Stories about the deceased or the relatives. Would you be up for that Sarah?"

"I ... I guess so."

"I'll start." Tom volunteered. He looked directly at Sarah. "I've never told you exactly how I came to live with your father two years ago."

Sarah leaned forward. She'd been wondering about that but then things happened so fast she never got a chance to ask him.

"When my mother became ill with ALS, and could no longer do anything for herself, your father was the only one in Broken Bow who would come around and visit. While she was still able to talk, he would be there for hours behind closed doors. I could hear her laughing and sometimes just giggling. I'd never heard my mother so happy."

Sarah didn't even know her father knew Mrs. Pawlak.

Tom looked around the room. "My father was a violent man when he got drunk. He often beat my mother for nonsensical reasons, and when he was done with her he beat me. The day he died was a release for both of us. But I had never heard my mother laugh until Mr. Cosgrave came visiting."

"How long ago was that?" Sarah asked.

"He started visiting five years ago and kept visiting until the day she died…two years ago." He swallowed hard. It was easier, but he still missed his mother. He wished he could have made her laugh instead of wandering the country—running away.

"Within a week after the funeral, the landlord kicked me out of the house. Though I'd been working and paying the rent the entire time my mother was sick, he said he had a buyer." Tom took Sarah's hands in his. "Your dad took me in immediately and offered me a place to stay in the barn at no charge. All I had to do was some work on the farm. That's the kind of man he was. That's the kind of man to remember and be proud of."

"But why did Mr. Pawlak come around all the time?" Kat asked. "Did you know him before? Was he a friend of your family?"

Tom chuckled. "Well, that's a more complicated story. I take it ya'll know about what an idiot I was seven years ago with Sarah?"

Everyone nodded. "Well, when Sarah told him about it and I tried to come back and make up, he met me with a gun and told me if I ever came on his land he'd shoot me. So we weren't the best of friends."

"That was the first time he ever stood up for me," Sarah said. "So, I still don't understand why he let you back."

"I think when he was visiting my mom, he could see that I'd changed." Tom said. "I believe he knew, more than most, what it was like to make mistakes you regretted. He always regretted that he couldn't quit drinking. Maybe seeing me turn my life around gave him hope, I don't know."

Tom drew an envelope out of his pocket and handed it to Sarah. "And this. I've been meaning to share this with you at the right time. This is something he wrote to my mother in her last week of life. It explains their relationship and shows what an honorable man your father was."

The room went quiet. Even the two children looked up as if sensing something important was about to happen. Sarah's hand shook as she took the envelope. Another secret? She scanned the contents and the tears she thought were gone reappeared.

Kat kneeled in front of her. "Are you okay? Is it good or bad?"

"Good," Sarah said and handed the letter to her. "You read it Kat so everyone can hear. I don't think I could get through it without crying."

Kat took it and turned to the group, sitting on the floor near Sarah and read aloud.

My Dearest Irena,

How is it we have waited so long to reconnect? It is the story of my life that I second guess myself, don't follow through, and don't feel worthy of anyone's love. Yet I have twice found true love, deserved or not. I am not a poet, or even a good writer, so I can't very well express in words how much these last two years together have meant. But I will try because in writing this down I can tell you what is in my heart, things that I would get tongue tied to say or stumble and forget.

I was stupid to have run from our relationship when we were in high school. I did love you then. You were my world and when I was with you I believed I could be anyone. Do anything. But then I would go home, and my father would remind me I was nothing. I'm afraid my father's voice won over yours. I couldn't guarantee that I could support you or care for you. I believed you deserved better. I believed that freeing you to find a better man was the only worthwhile thing I could offer. I am truly sorry for that, Irena. When I learned Tytus had gotten you pregnant, and you had married, I felt at fault there too for letting you down. I knew his reputation as a bully, yet I didn't warn you. It seems my life is full of sorrow in all my relationships.

Somehow, in spite of my mistakes, I found Lizzie and together we managed to make our sweet daughter Sarah. When Lizzie died I was so distraught I made a mess of everything with Sarah and with so many other women. I just wanted to stop the pain.

After the first few years, there were many times I thought of you. Many times when I dreamed of taking you and Tom and Sarah and running away from all our troubles. But I didn't know where to go. And I'd look at Sarah and wonder if I was betraying my love for Lizzie by even thinking of loving again. If only I could revisit all those decisions, I would make different ones. We would have had a decade together instead of only two years.

"OMG!" Kat interrupted her reading. "You and Tom could have been brother and sister!"

"Just read!" Michele and Rachel shouted together.

"Oh, right. Sorry." Kat turned back to the page. "Wow! This is like a movie or something. Like the one where— "

Everyone groaned.

"Okay. Okay."

WHEN TYTUS DIED, I was so happy for you. I thought again about coming to you and trying to reignite the flame. But by then I had even less to offer than before. I was an old man, a disgraced alcoholic, and I'd neglected the farm. I hadn't planted a crop in years, I lived on welfare and I owed everyone in town. I'd carefully constructed the perfect path straight to hell, and I didn't want to bring you down with me.

In my selfishness I never considered what you might want. I never considered even asking. I'm sorry I waited too long and that our time together now is so short. Thank you for loving me through everything that has happened.

I don't know how or why a hardened alcoholic has been blessed to find true love twice. All I know is that you have made this old man insanely happy for the past two years. I wish I could stop the progress of your disease and buy us more time. But I can't. I learned that with Lizzie. Death comes no matter what we do.

Perhaps my penance for all my sins is to watch those I love die before me. If so, it is the worst punishment anyone could devise. I suspect Hell will be a relief compared to this.

Now I've gone maudlin, and I promised myself I wouldn't do that. Irena, you have been a beacon of hope and happiness during our time together.

Thank you for who you are, for your acceptance of me in all my messiness. For both the laughter and the tears.

I do love you. I will stay with you and hold your hand until the very end. And, if possible, I will laugh in the face of death, just as you asked.

You will be in my heart always.

Love, Jack

KAT FOLDED the paper and handed it back to Sarah. "Did he laugh in the face of death, Tom?"

Tom grinned. "Sort of. He did it in his own way. When we took her ashes to the river, we each took turns scattering them. His first try, he stumbled on the slippery bank and some of the ashes landed on a Mississippi Kite as it swooped in to get a rat. The bird caught the rat in its talons and flew straight up to a nest in a nearby tree. Jack laughed and laughed at that. Then he shouted to the sky: 'See what happens, Irena? I'm not even drunk and I fall at your feet. I laugh at death, Irena. You vixen. I will see you in every damn Kite from now on.' "

Sarah laughed then too. She could picture him stumbling on the rocks. Trying so hard to do what was right. He might not have believed in God, but he understood other people's belief.

She put the letter back in the envelope and handed it to Tom. "Thank you. It makes me wish I had known your mother."

He squeezed her hand. "I wish you had too."

Just then Claire crawled into Noel's lap. "Daddy, I'm tired."

Michele stood and picked up a sleeping Tamara. "I think we need to get back to the hotel."

Sarah stood. "Of course. The time has really gone fast, hasn't it?"

Michele leaned in to hug Sarah. "We'll all be back tomorrow to have breakfast with you, then we have to get back on the road."

David gathered all the baby things together and slung the bag over his shoulder. "We're booked through August again. Almost every weekend, and a couple of midweek shows too," he said. "I'm still setting up more gigs and trying to hit up all the major festivals."

"I wish I was going with you," Sarah said. "I'm ready to get back to my guitar. I'm ready to get on with my life. I just need to sort things out with the house and ... " She looked over to Tom. "And some personal stuff too."

"Take your time," Theresa said. "We're managing without you, though it's not the same. Know we all want you back in the band—whenever you are ready."

Rachel gave her a hug too and whispered in her ear. "He's hot. Think about bringing him along with you."

Sarah blushed but couldn't help giggling either. "I'm trying to work it out. I'll keep you posted."

Kat was the last one to give her a hug. "I'm sending you the DVD of *The Princess Bride*," she said. You can be Buttercup and Tom can be Inigo Montoya."

"That could be interesting," Sarah said, chuckling at the picture in her head. "I'll bet he's never seen it."

Kat pumped her fist. "Yes. Score."

CHAPTER 10

SARAH PULLED OUT ANOTHER DRAWER from her father's dresser and poured it onto the bed. In the past week, she'd been going through all of his things and she had to admit that, so far, there wasn't anything she wanted to keep. His clothes were at least a decade old, tattered and worn through. Even Goodwill wouldn't take them in this shape.

In terms of furniture, it was the same furniture her mother had brought with her when they married. That meant it was at least thirty years old. The couch was lumpy, the beds had broken springs, all the side tables, nightstands, and even the dining room table were broken somewhere and patched together just enough to barely stand. If her mom hadn't inherited the house, she suspected her father would have been homeless.

How did she not know this? Growing up, she thought their home was normal. But then she didn't go visiting other kids much to compare. Instead, she always hurried home from school to do chores and take care of Dad.

She sat among the pieces of her father's life spread out on the bed. A movie ticket stub from fifteen years ago. A bill he never paid from last year. Nothing useful, except to reinforce that his life was always one of just barely getting by. She scooped it all into the trash. One more drawer to go, some cleaning, and then she could put the whole farm on the market.

She tugged hard. This drawer was heavy, and of course it was on the bottom. When it came loose she fell backwards. It was full of yellowed photo albums.

The first album she took out was clearly labeled *Lizzie and Jack*. She opened it to the first page. Wedding photos. She remembered these in frames over the fireplace. When did Dad take them down? When did he put them in an album? She never knew these existed. Did he take them out at night when she was in bed? Or did he hide them away until he thought he could handle them?

She ran her index finger over each picture, memorizing her mother's face. It was so long ago, and Dad had never offered her any pictures. She thought he had forgotten. But now … she had this. She hugged the album to her chest. "Thanks, Daddy. Thanks for taking the time to save these."

She went through each album in order. Her mother had chronicled every part of their lives from the time they were married until just before she died. There were lots of pictures of Sarah with her mother, only a few with her father. But when he was in the picture, they seemed to be having a great time. Why didn't she remember any of those times?

Then she took out the last album. This one was different. Instead of a basic white that had yellowed, this one had a cover with bright flowers and there was no label on the front.

She opened it carefully. She squinted at the faded picture. It looked like her dad, only really young. Underneath, in a neat script someone had written *first date with Jack*. She took the book over to a brighter light. The woman next to him was smiling and full of life. Could that be her mother? It must be but there was nothing about her that she remembered. Her mother was blonde. This woman seemed to be a brunette. They were probably near the same age.

On the same page were more photos. One with the woman

wearing shorts and leaning against a tree at a river. Another with her dad clowning around in the water, also wearing shorts.

"Oh!" She set the book aside not wanting to believe her eyes. Then she picked it up again. It was. It had to be Tom's mother, Irena. This must have been when they were in high school. But why did her father have this photo album? It was obviously Irena's, the photos were all labeled in a woman's handwriting.

She set it aside to ask Tom later. Maybe when his mother died, Dad wanted to keep it? Would Tom want it now?

TOM KNOCKED on the door and when he heard no response, he opened it and walked into the front room. "Sarah?" He raised his voice and called again. "Sarah?" He wandered down the hall.

She sat on her father's bed surrounded by photo albums. The one in her lap was open and she was just staring at it, not moving. He touched her lightly on the shoulder. "Sarah? Are you okay?"

"It's all true," she said, not looking up.

"What's true?" He took a seat beside her. "Can I see?"

She nodded and handed him the album. He started at the beginning. "That's … oh my god, that's my mother and your father."

"You didn't know about this?"

He shook his head and turned to the next page. More pictures, this time at some kind of formal event, like a prom. Then later camping with friends. There were no dates, just captions like *Spring Dance, Sadie Hawkins, Church Campout.*

"It looks like they were really an item in high school. When do you think that first date was? When they were fifteen? Sixteen?"

He looked again at that first picture. "I don't know. I mean I knew they had dated. When your dad starting spending so much time with mom in those last two years, she told me they were old friends. That they knew each other from high school. But I didn't know anything more until the letter. I found the letter in my mother's dresser next to the bed after she died."

He turned to Sarah and looked her in the eye. "Does it bother you? That they loved each other before your mother and dad got together?"

Her eyes looked over to a corner of the room for a minute, then back to him. "I'm not sure. I mean, everyone has a before life. The before-he-met-my-mom life. I'm just surprised that neither of us knew. I'm surprised that Dad had this with all the other albums."

"Mom must have given it to him. They probably went through it together and as she became sicker, she probably just gave it to him."

"Yes. That must be it." She sat very still. Then her shoulders fell, just a little.

"What?" He took her hand in his. "There's something else. What is it, Sarah?"

"It's silly. I'm just being selfish."

"You can tell me." He rubbed the back of her hand.

"It's just that it makes me wonder if he loved your mom more, you know, more than mine." She shifted away. "I know it doesn't really matter. It was before and it was after, and he deserves to be happy. But I can't help wondering if he just held a candle for your mom all the time my parents were married."

"Come here, Sarah." He pulled her to his side. "I think it is exactly as your father said in the letter. He was blessed to have two true loves in his life."

"But what if he hadn't run away. Or what if they had found each other again, like you and me, then would he have married your mom?"

"You can't get caught up in what-ifs. You can only go with what is or what was." He turned her so he could see her full face. "Though I wouldn't wish what my mom went through with my dad on anyone, I'm glad at this moment that they didn't get married."

"You are? Why?"

"Because if you were my sister, I wouldn't want to do this."

He framed her face with his hands and fluttered her lips with a passing kiss. She closed her eyes, and he lightly brushed each lid. In that moment, neither of them moved. Neither of them breathed, they just existed together.

Then her lips parted and he leaned into her and kissed her, slowly, reverently, still unbelieving they had found each other again. The silken fall of her hair glided across his hands as she pushed back and returned a kiss of aching sweetness. Then she wrapped her arms around his neck and gave into it, gave all to it, a moment's madness where her body ruled his mind and blood roared over reason.

He bent her head back across his arm and increased the intensity until both their lips were shaking. They clung to each other as if they were the only solid thing in the room. His insistent tongue darted in and out. Then he moved to her shoulder, pulling aside her T-shirt. He wanted to feel her skin. His hand snaked beneath the hem of her shirt and moved up her back as he deepened the kiss further.

"Stop. Please!" she whispered, turning her head from him.

He pressed her head hard against his shoulder and tamped down on the tremors of sensation that were driving him. "I've wanted to do this for years," he said. "You unhinge me, Sarah. When you kiss me like you just did, I don't want to stop. I want to drive you senseless, I want to see you completely wild."

She panted in short breaths against his shoulder. "You've succeeded," she finally said. "My head is spinning so fast, I don't know which way is up." She pushed herself just a few inches away, but then melted back against him. "You make me tingle all over. It's as if my blood is rushing to join yours. It's scary and exhilarating at the same time."

She slowed her breathing and stood up from the bed. "I don't want to stop either," she said. "I want to know what it feels like to completely let go, but one of us has to be responsible. It's not fair to always make me be the one to pull away."

Tom ran his fingers through his hair, needing to give them something else to do if they couldn't touch her. He looked at the photo album still open on the bed. "You're right." He moved toward the door and stood in the frame turned toward her. "It's not fair. But every time I'm near you, it seems that I can't help myself. I should leave."

"No!" She stood and took his hand. "I mean…you don't need to go. We just need to cool down."

"I don't know, Sarah."

"Please." She took the photo album and placed it back on the dresser. "Dinner? There is still so much food left."

He hesitated. He could stay for dinner. For two years he'd prepared dinner for Jack. He didn't have food in his little studio in the barn. He'd been trying to give Sarah space—space to decide what next steps were. "Okay," he said taking her hand and pulling her out of the bedroom and back toward the kitchen.

"There are things I want to talk about over dinner."

Tom raised his eyebrow. "Like?"

"Not now," she said. "I have to get my thoughts together. We'll talk over dinner. Okay?"

When they got to the kitchen, Tom started setting the table as Sara rooted in the refrigerator.

"Mac and cheese?" she asked. "I think we can finally finish it."

"That's good."

She handed out the dish to him. Then she pulled another one forward. "And green beans with mushrooms and topped with fried French onions and I'm not sure what else."

"Sounds like a comfort food night," he said.

She turned to him with the green bean dish. "Yes. I'm pretty sure it's all comfort food."

"Any of that apple pie left?"

She reached to the top of the refrigerator and pulled down a box. "I'm betting there is at least one piece."

"I'll try to share," he said with a smile. "Sounds like a perfect meal. Best part, neither one of us has to cook."

SARAH PLAYED with her piece of pie. She'd successfully avoided any really serious conversation during the main part of the meal and Tom hadn't pushed it. She took a big breath and let it out.

"What is it, Sarah."

"I...I've been thinking about what's next." There she'd said it. It was finally out there.

"The biggest thing you need to decide is what you want to do about the farm and the house," he said.

"Oh…" She hadn't thought it through. In her fairy tale mind, she figured she'd sell the farm, go back to Portland and somehow Tom would come with her. Easy. Simple. But now, she realized it was up to her whether to put Tom out of a home or not.

"Don't worry about me," Tom said, breaking the silence. "I can find another place to live."

Sarah looked at her pie and forked another piece. "Where?" She finally asked, abandoning the pie and pushing it aside. "You've been here for two years. Where would you go?"

"Do you want to keep the house and farm?" Tom asked, his eyes looking straight at her, unflinching.

"I…I'm not sure. I mean I…I live in Portland. I have a career as a musician. I…um…I'm not a farmer."

Her heart broke a little as she realized that she had been naïve to think that Tom would leave everything in Oklahoma and simply move to Portland. They'd only just reconnected and their relationship, despite the obvious attraction and rekindled memories, was nowhere near the commitment phase where one person moved out of state with another.

"I understand," Tom finally said. "But the question still stands, do you want to keep the farm or sell it?"

"What do *you* want to do?" she whispered. "Do you want to stay here? Do you want to be a farmer?" She held her breath, afraid of the answer.

He sighed and looked over her head. "No."

Her eyes widened and she let hope in. "No?"

"No," he repeated. "I was forced to be a farmer growing up. I did it here to help out Jack. But it's not my passion. It's a hard life —one where you're never sure if the crop will come in, if the weather will be right, if the markets will be up or down. It's an honest life, but a life you have to love to do it into old age. I don't love it. That's why I got a business degree. My emphasis was in marketing."

"What kind of business do you want to be in?" she asked. "Do *you* want to stay here in Broken Bow or somewhere else?"

"I don't know yet. When I made the commitment to stay with Jack, I just kind of put it off. I knew it would be at least a couple of years. Now I have a chance to figure that out. To finally put my degree to good use."

Did she dare hope he would move to Portland? That they would have a chance at a real relationship in the town she now called home?

"I don't…" they said simultaneously.

Sarah laughed. "You first."

Tom reached across the table and took her hand. "I don't think our relationship, our trust is to the point where I can follow you to Portland."

Sarah swallowed. How did he know what she'd been thinking? Hoping. She knew that he was right. It wasn't what she wanted to hear but it was true. Even though her feelings were strong, there was no way she would stay here just for Tom—give up Sweetwater Canyon and her career. So, she couldn't expect that of him either.

"I…understand."

"You need to get back to the band, to your friends. I'll help you get set up with a good real estate agent. I'll stay here until the farm sells to make sure things are kept up."

"You don't need to do that," she said. "It's my problem."

Tom stood and took his dishes to the sink. "Let me do this. I owe Jack. I owe you. I've lived here for two years free."

She joined him at the sink, automatically drying the dishes as he washed them. "Not free. You worked for your room and board."

"I did it gladly. For Jack. And now I would like to do it for you." Tom turned to her. "Sarah, let me do this. It will give me time to find a place and it will give you a way to get back to your career faster. It may take months for this place to sell. You can't afford to be gone from the band that long."

She finished drying the last dish, afraid to look into Tom's eyes. Afraid to see if he had already given up on a long-term relationship. Did he recognize this might be the end? Even if they loved each other, any reasonable person would know that living two-thousand miles apart would put a strain on the best of relationships. And this relationship was really new, untested, restarted in the midst of grief and confusion. Maybe they didn't really love each other. Maybe it was just all mixed up in everything that happened in the past, with her dad, with his family. Maybe...

"Earth to Sarah," Tom said to her back.

She turned slowly. "Just wool gathering."

"Uh huh. How about we gather together instead of alone?"

She cocked her head to one side and looked up at him. "I'm stuck. I'm not sure where things are going with us. I can't stay here but I don't want to leave. I know you will do everything to take care of the farm, but..."

He gathered her into his arms. "I love you. If you think of nothing else, think of that."

She sighed into his chest. It was what she wanted to hear. But she knew that love wasn't always enough.

"We will figure this out," he said.

She nodded against his chest. Her eyes misted at the thought of leaving. He was right. She needed to get back. Sweetwater Canyon had already started touring. They'd done six gigs without her and she couldn't expect Theresa to keep picking up her load.

"A week," she mumbled into his chest. "You're right. I need to stop dawdling and get on with life. I'll make my plans to rejoin the band in a week. That should be enough time to get everything set with the realtor. Sweetwater Canyon will be in the Midwest by then. They are booked for two weeks in Branson."

"Sounds like a good plan." His voice seemed far away.

She wrapped her arms around his waist and hugged tighter. "Yes. A good plan."

THE WEEK FLEW BY. Between cleaning the entire house, fixing lots of little problems with plumbing and electrical, and caulking. It seemed like every surface needed some kind of caulking. She and Tom had worked side by side through it all. He helped her inside the house, and she helped him with the farm outside.

The farm was all consuming. Even with new plants already in, it still took a lot of work. They were up by 6am and already outside. Kip followed them everywhere. Lots of watering. All the watering was done by hand, row after row. Her father could never afford any type of automatic irrigation. Then the weeding began, including picking bugs off the plants. Growing organic meant no spraying. They did do companion planting to keep away as many bugs as possible. Herbs like yarrow, citronella, mint, lemongrass and fennel were planted along with the rows of vegetables. But with things barely germinating now, those hadn't grown enough to be of use yet. And there was the mulching too. By the time they both retired around 10pm, it was all Sarah could do to find her way into the shower and into bed.

She had no idea how Tom had managed the farm for two years while taking care of her father and working another job at night. Even with the two of them it was more work than she'd done in her life. Crazy. And crazy lucky he had three weeks off to make sure everything was started just right. It would help the resale if other farmers saw the care of the crops and knew how to market organic like Tom did.

Every day she learned something new about the man Tom had become. He was responsible. He was a good man. A man who took his time and did things right. He didn't cut corners with his repairs. He always took time to play with the dogs. He still retained his sense of humor; and the ease she had felt with him as a friend was there just as much as it had been before. Only now it was more than friendship.

Sarah stretched as she finished the last row of weeding. When she turned she caught Tom watching her. He smiled and waved from the pasture where he'd been feeding the two horses.

"What are you looking at," she asked as she walked toward him.

"You. And your cute butt."

She felt her cheeks redden. She still wasn't comfortable with a man not only noticing her body but also commenting on it. "Sounds dangerous," she countered, trying for nonchalance.

He nodded and one side of his mouth quirked up in a smirk. "Yup, your butt is definitely dangerous."

"How would you know?"

"I can tell just by looking."

She had no response to that.

"I can prove it too," he offered.

"Um…I don't think that would be wise." She stayed a couple steps away from him. He always kept her off guard with his suggestive talk. On the one hand she liked it. She could definitely admit to herself that she thought of him in that way. On the other hand, it scared her to death because she knew where it could lead.

"I'm going to jump in the shower and then come over for dinner. Is that okay with you?"

"Of course." She nodded. "But we're out of leftovers from the funeral."

"No problem. I stopped by the store early this morning to stock up for myself. I'll cook."

She smiled. "I'll never turn away a good cook."

"Good, see you in ten minutes or so then." As he walked behind her toward the barn he gave her butt a little pat.

She turned quickly, but he was already out of reach. He was chuckling as his pace picked up. "Cute butt," he called back over his shoulder.

She shook her head as she headed back to the house to take a shower too. The past week had brought them so close to making love. Each time she'd been the one to pull away. Each time she reminded herself that she was saving herself for marriage and that, given the circumstances they faced, there was little guarantee Tom would ever be her husband.

She wished she could be more free with her flirting. She had been more open, unrestricted in high school. Of course, that was before she really knew what it all might lead to. Back then she didn't worry about the future. She didn't have to make plans. She just had fun with

Tom. She'd enjoyed being around him and loved the sensation of her skin tingling every time he touched her, every time his lips found hers she saw a future together that she never questioned. But she wasn't that young naïve girl anymore. Now she questioned everything.

They never talked about the future now. It was almost as if they'd had a silent agreement not to look too far ahead. Worrying about it would take time away from the work and the ease they had found with each other. Talking about it might bring questions or answers they didn't want to hear.

But now their time was up. Tomorrow morning Tom would take her to the airport and say goodbye. She would rejoin her band. Tom would move into the house until it sold. Then he would find a permanent job in business. Maybe not in Broken Bow, but he'd never mentioned living in Oklahoma. She couldn't ask him to move to Portland.

She sighed with resignation as she stripped out of her dirty clothes and stepped into the shower. She quickly soaped up and cleaned all the grime of the day away. As the warm water sluiced over her back and rinsed away the soap she leaned her forehead on the wall and wondered if she was making the right decision. What if she never found the right man? She'd been trying for seven years and not been successful. What if the one man she truly loved would never be available to her and she would never experience that sexual kind of love that she craved with him.

Lord, what am I doing here? Why did you put Tom in my path again only to take him away? I want him so badly, in every way and now it seems I will lose him again. I know I love him and he loves me. Is it really so wrong to sleep with him before I leave? I don't think I can pass up the chance twice. Without him in my life, I may never marry. I want...no I need...this last night to mean something special for both of us. Please let me have this last night to hold in my memory for all my days.

She waited quietly, trying to listen to her heart. Trying to believe that God understood and that, knowing the future, He would give His blessing. Then the water suddenly turned cold. She yelped and turned off the faucet. "Not fair," she yelled at the ceiling. "Definitely not fair."

CHAPTER 11

SARAH OPENED THE DOOR. Tom stood on the porch with a bouquet of daisies in one hand and a bag of groceries in the other. The jeans he wore looked new and like they were made especially for his body. They conformed nicely to his muscular thighs. His favorite Oklahoma State University t-shirt stretched taut across his wide chest.

She gulped and reached for the flowers. "Thank you. I'll put these in water." She held the door open and gestured him toward the kitchen. "You know where everything is. Make yourself at home."

"I will." He smiled and brushed a kiss on her cheek as he passed by.

She watched him saunter to the kitchen. That butt was perfect. She swallowed and gathered her courage. "Cute butt," she called out.

He laughed and kept walking.

She opened and closed each dish cupboard looking for a flower vase. She couldn't remember seeing one in all their cleaning. Finally, she settled on a water pitcher instead. She quickly filled it with water, arranged the flowers, and then placed them on the dining table at the other end of the kitchen.

When she returned to his side, he'd already started chopping a variety of vegetables. As he finished each one, he placed it into its own bowl. Then he moved on to chopping an onion and some mushrooms. "What are you doing?" She asked.

"*Mise en place*," he said.

"Meez what?"

"*Mise en place* is a French cooking term which means to have all your ingredients prepared and ready to go before you start cooking. Translated, 'to put in place'."

"I didn't know you spoke French."

"I don't, but I love to cook."

"Well, it happens I love to eat." She giggled with a bit of giddiness. "Can I do anything?"

"Yes. Could you get the rice started? It's in a canister in the pantry. One cup should be more than enough."

"Two to one?" She asked.

"Right. Two cups water to one cup rice. Should take about fifteen minutes."

Sarah busied herself with boiling water and tending the rice while Tom finished cutting everything. He then placed all the bowls on the counter to the right of the stove.

Next he put out the acrylic cutting board and set out meat strips. The knife clicked precisely as he sliced them into bite-sized pieces.

"Looks like pork," she said.

"I thought stir fry would be good tonight. I hope you like stir fry."

"Are you kidding? It's one of my favorites. And after all that comfort food we've been eating, something a little healthy would be wonderful."

Wok. She had seen a wok somewhere, but where? It certainly wasn't something her father had when she was a child. In fact, she couldn't even remember her father ever cooking—except TV dinners.

She looked up and saw it on top of a small crate on top of the refrigerator. She stood on her toes and reached, her fingers barely grazing it but not able to get purchase.

"Let me."

Her breath caught as she felt Tom behind her, his thighs and chest pressing her slightly toward the refrigerator. His arm brushed over her outreached one as he grasped the wok and easily removed it from the top. As he pulled it down he placed his other hand around her waist and pulled her against him.

"I've got you now," he whispered into her ear. "I'm not letting go."

She leaned into him and turned her head slightly to one side, arching her neck. "I don't want you to let go. Ever."

He shifted to one side, never releasing his hand from her back, and placed the wok on the counter next to all the bowls. His freed hand then caressed her jaw before he leaned in, his breath warm upon her mouth. Neither one spoke. It was as if he held her in a sensuous stasis. The warmth of his breath slowly melting away every last shred of steadiness she'd stored.

When she thought she could wait no more, she lifted her fingers to his jaw, and he finally lowered his mouth inch by torturous inch until his lips pressed softly against hers. Ever so slowly he held her lower lip between his. Then he moved from one corner to the next, his lips paving an addictive path to her upper lip, only to repeat his exploration. She dared not move for fear this most extraordinary pleasure would end. Then once again he pressed his lips at the center of both hers and slowly lifted from her.

She wasn't sure how long she stood there waiting before she opened her eyes, only to be mesmerized once more by his chocolate stare piercing straight to her heart.

"I won't lose you again," he said. "I can't."

She had no words, only more emotion than she knew what to do with safely.

The stove timer dinged, shattering the moment.

"The rice!" She brushed past him to turn off the burner and move the rice to a cooler spot. "Dinner?"

He chuckled as he set the wok on a ring on the stovetop, added oil, and turned the burner on. "I guess I got a little distracted."

"You think?"

Over the next ten minutes, she handed him ingredients as he stirred them in. First the pork, and then each bowl coming in a specific order. In the last two minutes he added a variety of pre-

prepared sauces. Sarah leaned closer to the wok to breathe in the aromas. "Smells magnificent."

He turned it off and pulled down two plain white plates. "If you'll serve the rice, I'll top it with stir fry."

Within minutes dinner was on the table and Tom was laughing at Sarah's attempt to use chopsticks.

"I've never learned how to do this," she said, dropping yet another vegetable before it reached her mouth. I'm getting a fork or I'll starve. She took three long steps to the counter and grabbed a fork and knife out of the drawer.

When she sat again, Tom deftly reached over and picked up a piece of pork and a little rice with his chop stocks. He held it to her lips. "The trick is getting the rice, too."

She opened her mouth to take his offer. "Mmmm. Food." He offered another bite. "Good."

He chuckled. "Your words of love are endearing."

"Hey, I'm starving here. Single syllables are all I can get out."

He offered her another bite. This time she let it sit on her tongue so she could enjoy the medley of tastes: a complex smoky, singed flavor with a tang of sweetness and citrus, while simultaneously retaining a crisp, fresh crunch of vegetables. "You really are good. I should have given in and let you do the cooking when I first arrived. It would have been so much better than what I was doing."

"You weren't exactly so trusting then," he reminded as he scooped a bite into his mouth.

He was right. She'd come in with an attitude of no one being trustworthy except herself. From the beginning she lacked compassion for her father. She didn't give Tom a chance to explain what happened. She was quick to believe the worst of him and her father. She'd been pretty rough on him until recently.

"I'm sorry for being such a jerk."

"You're forgiven."

She stopped eating for a moment and sat up straight. She had never thought she'd be the one needing forgiveness.

"Sarah?" Tom was staring at her again. "Something wrong."

"I just realized something about myself—something that isn't very Christian at all. Are you familiar with Proverbs 16:18?"

Tom cleared his throat. "I'm…uh…not a church goin' man. Haven't been to church since high school and can't imagine going back. Even in childhood I never found any solace there. People in this town knew my dad was beating the crap out of Mom and me but they did nothing. When Mom would take me to church, no one sat with us. It was like they were afraid if they talked to us it would rub off on them or something."

Sarah's heart stumbled a little at that response. How could she be in love with someone who didn't believe? She thought back to the verse. "It says: Pride goes before destruction, and a haughty spirit before a fall."

"Yeah I've heard something similar: 'pride goes before a fall. What does that have to do with you? You've never struck me as a prideful woman. You were always kind to me, open. You always trusted me to the best person possible."

Sarah took more bites of her meal as she measured her response. "When I was young, I guess I was that way. But after I left here, I let all my anger eat away at me. I used you and my dad as an excuse to distance myself from people. I judged everyone against some perfect standard."

"Some of us deserved judging," Tom said as he took her hand and ran his thumb across the back of it. "I certainly did. So did your father."

"But not by me," she said. "By God, not me. And it wasn't just you. I judged my band mates too. I judged Michele when she fought with David. I judged Theresa when I thought she was raising Kat too liberally. I particularly harshly judged one of my band mates because she slept with a lot of men."

"I can understand that," Tom said. "Sleeping around tends to show bad judgment."

"But it's even worse than that. When she was raped, I judged her too. It wasn't that I thought she deserved it. No one deserves what happened to her. It was just that I figured she set herself up…

or that it would never happen to me because I didn't sleep around."

Tom was silent, but he still held tight to her hand.

"I've been so busy judging everyone and holding myself and my behavior above them, that I don't really know anything about relationships—building them, keeping them, going through hard times together, understanding all the messiness. I've done a great job of avoiding messiness at all cost."

He stood and came around the table to her side. He kneeled on one knee in front of her. "All of us have things to be ashamed of. Don't also judge yourself too harshly, Sarah."

She shook her head. "I've been a self-righteous..." She couldn't even finish the sentence without uttering a bad word. "Well, it stops now. I'm going to embrace messiness from now on. Life is messy and I will learn to accept that."

Tom stood. "Our relationship certainly has its share of messiness."

Sarah nodded. She wanted to say it was okay and she was ready to move forward. She did still love him and she did want to be with him...but...she wasn't sure what she was willing to give up for that. She shook her head. She couldn't deal with it now. It was still messy.

"Speaking of messiness," she said. "The kitchen is a mess. I have dibs on washing this time." She handed him the drying towel hanging on the rack since lunch. "You dry."

She filled the sink with soapy water and then stacked the dishes to one side in the order she would wash them. Glasses first, followed by all those ingredient bowls, then plates and silverware. The wok was last. She was glad to have something to do instead of letting her mind spin in circles.

When they'd finished neither of them moved from the sink. She turned and wrapped her arms around Tom's waist, settling her head on his chest. She didn't want the night to end. She didn't want tomorrow to come. She wasn't ready. Her eyes misted with the thought of having to leave. She squeezed them shut to close off the tears.

Tom rubbed comforting circles on her back. "It's hard for me too."

She took a step back and looked up at him. "Is it?"

"I ache with the thought of you leaving." He drew her closer and lowered his forehead to balance against hers. "I will miss having you around. I will miss coming out of my apartment and knowing I'll be having breakfast with you. I'll miss sharing the chores with you, cooking with you, arguing with you, laughing with you."

Her skin quivered as his soft fingertips brushed errant strands of hair from her face.

"Do you know how hard it is to know I won't be able to do this?" His lips brushed across her forehead and his eyelashes feathered across her hairline causing tingles along her scalp and down her spine. Her weighted eyelids lowered.

"And this." His hands gently cupped her jaw, his thumbs caressing her cheeks as he kissed each eyelid. Her heartbeat quickened and energy flushed her pores. She inhaled his grass-scented hair. A soft moan escaped her lips, her thoughts lost in delicious amnesia. Slowly, tinder ignited as he nibbled her lower lip slowly.

She couldn't help but open to him, her tongue automatically licking everywhere his lips had touched. As she withdrew, his tongue followed hers inside, darting in and out with a feathered touch, drawing her further into his kiss. Then he captured her tongue between his lips and withdrew slowly. As her legs melted beneath her, he pulled her into his chest, supporting her weight. His hands caressed her neck as he pushed aside her long hair and kissed her softly behind her ear.

"I'm stopping now." He moaned the words into her ear. "You don't have to be the one to always say stop."

She knew she should thank him. But she couldn't find the words. She didn't want this to end. "Stay," she said.

"Sarah." He dipped his lips to her again and she returned his passion greedily, her hands raking down his back as she leaned deeper into the kiss.

He pulled away and held her head firmly against his chest, his breathing rapid. She could hear his heart pounding faster.

"Sarah, you don't want this. You said you wanted to wait."

She could barely catch her own breath. "I know. I do. But I don't."

His chest rumbled as he chuckled and his breathing slowed.

"I…don't want to spend my last night here alone, without you," she said. "I don't know exactly what that means. Please. Stay."

He led her to the sofa and sat, tucking her into his side, his arm firmly around her. With the other hand he pulled the afghan over both of them. "I'll spend the night with you." He fluttered a kiss across her scalp, then deftly turned on the television and flipped through the channels.

She sighed and snuggled in closer. "Find us a love story, Tom. One that ends perfectly."

He settled on a classic movie channel playing *The Shop Around the Corner* with Jimmy Stewart and Margaret Sullavan.

SARAH WATCHED the planes landing and taking off again as she waited at a small table facing the runway. Tom had left her to look for coffee and a sweet roll, and she was wondering how she could say goodbye without crying. Too much was up in the air. Too much was still unknown. Was it really possible they could make a life together when they lived so far apart?

They'd filled the two-hour drive to the airport with business talk. How they would stay in touch. How he'd update her at least once a week with sale prospects. What he'd be doing around the farm to make sure it showed well and would be of interest to a buyer.

She'd checked her luggage, except her guitar and a small carry-on bag. She usually traveled to gigs aboard Annabelle, the RV that the band used when traveling. Though the new airline regulations said musical instruments could be taken onboard, if they fit in the overhead compartment or under the seat, she wasn't taking any chances. She'd purchased the seat next to her for her guitar. Her dreadnought was large and, depending on the type of plane, it didn't always fit in the overhead. Not to mention that she didn't want to compete with luggage being pushed in next to it, or worse on top of it. Also, placing her guitar in the middle seat guaranteed she wouldn't be next to an unruly seat partner. The way she felt right now, she wouldn't be in the mood to talk to any strangers.

"What's going on in that head?" Tom asked as he put the steaming coffee in front of her, brushed her cheek with a glancing kiss, and slid into the seat next to her. "Are you already planning your songs? Strumming your guitar with Sweetwater Canyon."

They didn't know what would happen next. They couldn't make promises. She knew this was not going to be one of those movie scene romantic partings with promises of a life together no matter what. But, darn it that is exactly what she wanted from him just before she got on the plane.

"I'm already missing you," she finally said.

"I'm right here. I'm not going anywhere." Tom gently placed his hand on her jean-clad thigh.

"I know, but…"

"No buts, Sarah. Let's get through selling the house and you getting back on the road. Then will decide how I can join you."

She turned to face him. "I can't ask you to do that, to leave Broken Bow and move to Portland, a place you've never been and don't know if you'd even like."

"You're not asking me, I want to be with you. I can live anywhere if it's with you."

"I don't know." She took a long sip of coffee. "There's all the time on the road too."

"Didn't you tell me that Rachel's and Michele's husbands sometimes come on the road?"

"Yes, but…"

"There is that but again. Don't you want me with you?"

She leaned into him. "Of course I do. I just want you to be doing something that is meaningful to you. Not just be a…a…"

"Hanger on? And here I thought I'd found myself a sugar mama."

She playfully punched him in the shoulder. "You know what I mean. Michele's husband is our manager and he has his own business still to run, something separate from the band. Rachel's husband is a teacher and he only joins us on school breaks.

"I'm afraid that if you move just for me, without a plan to do something you really want to do as a career, that eventually you'll hate me for luring you into the life of a roadie."

Tom chuckled and drew her close, his arm around her shoulder. "I didn't realize what a worrier you are. As for luring me, I agree with that. You lured me into your sphere when I was seventeen and I've been dying to be with you again. But give me some credit. I wanted to be lured and I'm not without skills to find my way wherever we end up."

She sighed. "I guess I just want things to be perfect."

"They'll never be perfect, Sarah. In fact, it is in struggling with imperfection that we will be stronger together."

"But we've already been through that part," she complained. "Don't we get the perfect for a little while?" She know she sounded whiney but she was tired, worried, scared to leave and scared to stay. She needed a little perfect.

He hugged her tight.

She glanced at the clock and sighed. "I need to get moving toward security. It's going to take awhile to get through the lines."

In silence they cleared the table and then walked hand in hand toward the checkpoint. Sarah hated goodbyes. Even when she ran from Broken Bow so many years ago, she never felt she'd had closure. And here she was again, leaving without Tom, leaving without assurances of what would come next.

"Looks the line isn't too bad." Tom gestured about fifty feet in front of them.

Sarah shrugged. "Maybe only a ten minute process."

Tom looked at his watch. "You still have an hour before you have to board. Come with me." He firmly put his arm around her waist and guided her out of the main foot traffic to a corner outside the main corridor.

He took her guitar and carry-on and carefully placed it next to them on the wall. He placed both hands on either side of her, effectively trapping her against the wall. She couldn't help but look up at him. She wanted to memorize the close cut hair, the broad chest. Shadows and light behind him swirled, merged as she inhaled his scent—a wild breeze mixed with the symphony of a light rain.

His face became blurry as it neared hers. He lowered his lips to hers, keeping both hands on the wall as he exhaled on a long coffee-laced breath. With his lips close to her ear he whispered, "You are my center, the light in my days. If I could go with you now I would without hesitation. I will miss you in every moment of the next few weeks. I will wake wondering why the sun isn't as bright. I will work on the farm knowing that soon we will be sharing our days and nights together. I love you, Sarah, and I will not let you go ever again."

The chaos of the terminal disappeared as she reveled in his words. Her hands rested lightly on his chest, not pushing him away.

His hands left the wall to cover the back of her hands. He pressed her palms into his chest and she could feel the beat of his heart thrumming through her finger tips and traveling up her arms. He dragged her hands up, wrapping them around his neck as his body slowly crowded closer. She had no fear as he pressed his body to her from knees to chest.

His fingers trailed down the undersides of her arms, then down her ribcage, coming to rest at her waist. They were pressed closer than ever before and every part of her arched toward him wanting to become one.

She couldn't help but open her lips in a tiny gasp as she felt him meld his lips to hers. But his lips weren't enough. She wanted the same air that he breathed. She wanted to tell him, with her mouth, exactly how she felt. She opened for him and he took full advantage.

His taste, his delicious, addictive taste exploded through her senses as he delved into her. She tentatively sucked his tongue and he plunged it deeper into her mouth. A low growl rumbled through him. Muscles tensed in his neck as the kiss intensified.

She needed more—more taste, more sensation, more of everything he promised. She lost herself in him. Their mouth and tongues speaking from the heart in a way words never would. She finally believed the words from Matthew that were often used in wedding vows. *What God has joined together let no man put asunder.*

Her faith in God had brought her to Broken Bow to face her past, and in doing so she'd regained Tom. She had no question they were meant to be one and that God would bless their marriage. They could no more spiritually separate from one another now than they could separate from themselves.

She prayed he felt the same.

CHAPTER 12

WITHIN A FEW MINUTES of walking off the plane, Sarah was inside the airport and rushed by Theresa, Kat, Rachel, and Michele all talking at once while simultaneously relieving her of her guitar and carry-on, then hugging and guiding her forward to pick up her luggage.

Once they were at the carousel waiting, Kat's voice broke through all the others. "Well? Share."

Everyone quieted and looked at Sarah.

Her cheeks grew hot. "Share what?"

Kat playfully punched her in the arm. "Tom, you nitwit. Are you back in love or is he a jerk after all? Will he be coming to any of our gigs like David did for Michele? The resort is really great to get romantic and all, and you have your own room. So, you know, tell all."

"Sarah doesn't tryst," Rachel said. "Remember. Virgin?"

Sarah fidgeted with her purse. She'd never been the one to talk about boyfriends. Not that there had been much to say except that a relationship didn't work out. She'd always kept to herself about personal matters. Her desire to not have sex until marriage had long been a topic of conversation with her band mates, especially Rachel who easily talked about sex.

"Hmmm…" Rachel cocked an eyebrow. "No virgin? Are congratulations in order?"

"No," Sarah said with finality. "I did not sleep with him."

"But?" Kat drew out the word.

Theresa pulled Kat back. "Oh leave her alone. She's barely arrived. She's had a tough few weeks. If she wants to tell us something, she will."

"Mom!" Kat protested. "She wants to tell. I can see it in her eyes." She turned back to Sarah. "But?"

Sarah looked around the circle of her friends. This was her family. The people who knew her and liked her anyway, even when they didn't agree. Even if she was the only twenty-six-year-old virgin in the world.

"But…" She spotted her two floral suitcases just starting down the luggage chute. "But I wanted to. Really bad." Then she sprinted away to retrieve her luggage.

Kat shouted, "I knew it. I knew it. Hey, where you going?"

Sarah couldn't help laughing as she hauled the two large suitcases off the carousel and rolled them back to her friends. It was good to be back with them. After seven years of dating and watching first Michele and then Rachel fall in love and get married, she thought it would never happen to her. Now she at least had some hope to share.

They hustled her out of the airport and onto a shuttle bus to the resort just outside of the city.

"No Annabelle to greet me?" She asked.

"Annabelle is parked in an RV lot," Theresa said. "We get real hotel rooms this time."

"Not soon enough for me," Kat chimed in. "You know how it is traveling for two weeks with everyone in that small space. It's nice to share my space only with Mom."

"David negotiated with the resort to provide rooms for us all because we're there for four weeks." Michele's voice held obvious pride for her husband. "And that means that David and Tamara can be here with me too."

Sarah turned to Rachel. "And Noel and Claire?"

"No, school's still in session," Rachel answered. "But they are flying out over Memorial Day weekend to spend time with us."

"So, being as I don't want you to be lonely..." Kat twirled her hair in a finger. "Any chance you want a roommate?"

"Careful what you wish for," Theresa said. "Sarah is probably even stricter than I am."

Kat jumped off the shuttle bus first with one of Sarah's bags. "At least I can check out your room. Then I'll decide."

"Really it's okay," Sarah told Theresa. "I like her energy. I'll make sure she stays in line."

"Your room is the smallest of all of ours because you are a single. We booked you with one queen bed. Believe me, you do not want to share that with Kat. First she'll talk your head off every night. Then her energy continues even when she's sleeping. I think she runs races in her dreams because she's always kicking off the covers, tossing and turning."

"I suspect when she sees there is only one bed she'll realize it won't work."

Theresa rolled her eyes and chuckled. "One never knows how her brain will take it in. She may even decide that camping out on the floor with you is better than having her own bed in a room with me."

SARAH WOKE SUDDENLY and checked the clock near her bed. Three in the afternoon. Thank goodness. She still had time to shower. When she'd finally shooed Kat out of her room and unpacked everything, she was so tired she decided to take nap for just a few minutes. She'd meant to set the alarm but, before she knew it, she was dead to the world.

Four o'clock would be the first time Sweetwater Canyon could get into the theater, check out the stage, do a sound check and maybe some rehearsing. This weekend and next they were only expected to play Friday and Saturday night. From Memorial Day until mid-June they were expected to play Wednesday through

Sunday. A two-hour set every night with a fifteen-minute intermission.

The resort theater held a little over two thousand people, so this was the biggest venue they'd ever played. It was also the first time they were booked for more than one weekend. In their eight years of touring, she'd given up on Sweetwater Canyon ever getting these kinds of gigs. But now, with five albums out and David coordinating and negotiating their tours, they'd gotten a bit of a reputation for good, wholesome family-friendly music with a message of hope.

Sarah had been so out of the loop the past couple of months that she didn't even know what was in the set list for these shows. She hoped every show wouldn't be exactly the same. Between the four of them, they had a good selection of about forty pieces of original music ranging from ballads to country and even a little bluegrass mixed with a rock sound. They rounded out their sets from a selection of thirty cover songs that served as good companion pieces.

After her shower and getting dressed, she took a few minutes to review the song she'd finally finished before everything changed in Oklahoma. They'd never had a chance to even rehearse it. In fact, she couldn't remember if she even gave it to them.

> *I close my eyes to draw you near.*
> *Teach me, Lord, to simply hear.*
> *Lead me through the muddy dark.*
> *Help me mend this broken heart.*

So much had changed since she'd penned those words. Her heart was now full instead of broken. The Lord had led her through the darkness of reconciling with her father, grieving his death, and forgiving Tom's past. Though that song was good she put it aside. It would have to wait for some other time, when she could look back to the person she was before she went back to Broken Bow. It might be after Branson. It might not be until a year or more before she would tackle it again.

Sarah looked at the clock. 3:50! She would be late if she didn't hurry. She grabbed her guitar and her music and tried to speed walk to the theater.

She arrived at the door two minutes before 4:00 and found everyone else waiting for her. A luggage cart, stacked with all of their instruments was also at the door.

"What's going on?" she asked, out of breath.

"Waiting for the key," Rachel answered.

"I guess when they say it will be open at four o'clock, they mean not a minute earlier," Kat said. "So, did you get a nap?"

Sarah nodded. "Where's David?"

"He's back at the room with Tamara," Michele said. "She's still napping and I didn't want to wake her. They might come over later though, or maybe just meet us for dinner."

"Any new music to share?" Rachel asked. "Before everything happened you said you had something new. We can still work it into the set list."

Just then a young man, not much older than Kat, rode up in a golf cart and hopped out.

"Not bad," Kat said under her breath next to Sarah.

Sarah elbowed her in the ribs. "Be good."

"Sweetwater Canyon?" the young man asked.

"Duh," Kat said pointing to all the instruments they had with them.

He smiled directly at Kat. "Just making sure some other band wasn't horning in on your time." He swiped the keylock at the door and it immediately clicked. He pushed the door inward until it fully opened and then kicked a doorstop under it.

"And are you the guy in charge of the sound mixer and lighting too?" Theresa asked before she walked through the door.

"That would be me. Randy Marshall at your service." He doffed his baseball cap to her with a slight bow. "Your microphones are already set up based on the diagram you sent with the contract." He took hold of the luggage cart. "Let's get all your instruments onto the stage and I'll give you the general tour."

The entire setup was larger than anywhere they'd ever played. On one side of the stage was a prep room with a variety of drinks—both alcoholic and non—on top of a sideboard along with the type of snacks you would usually find in a hotel fridge. Nuts, cheese, chocolate bars, everything that wasn't good for her diet. At the back of the room was a door that led to the bathroom and dressing area.

The adjoining bathroom and dressing room was decorated in what she would call modern country. At the back were two fully enclosed toilet stalls with fancy wood-trimmed doors. Along one side was the longest trough-type sink she'd ever seen with four faucets along its length. The mirror above it made the entire room seem even larger. At the center of this space were two winged-back chairs with a plaid print of reds, browns, and gold and a solid brown ottoman. The only thing missing was a chaise lounge.

When they finally made it onto the stage, Sarah felt quite small on it. She estimated it was at least forty feet across. She looked out to the auditorium and let out a whistle. "My goodness. I knew it was big but you just don't realize how that feels until you're up here."

"Yup," Randy came to her side. "It holds a little over two-thousand people without having a balcony."

"I don't think I want to think about that," she said. "It already scares me death."

"Don't worry," Kat said as she came up to the other side of Randy. "The lights will probably blind us. We won't be able to see anybody."

"That's mostly true," Randy agreed. "However, if you come to the front of the stage, you will see the first three rows or so. If you focus on your smaller space you'll be fine." He pointed to the center of the stage where a rug that was maybe fifteen to sixteen feet across defined a cozier space. The microphone stands were on that, along with a short stool for Theresa and a couple of smaller wooden tables placed near each microphone with water bottles.

Sarah walked over to the rug and took her place at her usual microphone. The one more toward the back of the shared space. "This feels better."

"Any chance you've marked up a set list with what you want for lighting? Do you need a follow spot, or just general mood lighting?"

"You can just follow me all the time," Kat said, pointing to herself. "I'm the most interesting."

Everyone laughed and Theresa said, "No doubt about that."

"As for mood, make it very moody," Kat added.

Randy laughed. "Got it."

"Actually, we're used to figuring it out the first night in rehearsal." Michele said. "Every venue is different and we like to get the feel of the room first."

"Not a problem. I'll be at the back of the room in that booth." He pointed to a large square that obviously held mixing equipment. "We can work out all the lighting with this rehearsal and I'll program it in. Then tomorrow we can go through the whole thing in dress and make sure I got it right."

The next few minutes were spent getting out instruments, tuning, setting them up on stage and just getting the feel of the space and the acoustics of the auditorium. Sarah looked over the set list and practiced a little with her guitar to remind her how some of the songs went.

Rachel stepped up to the microphone to Sarah's right. After tuning her violin she turned. "You ready to be back at it?"

Sarah nodded. "More than ready."

"All right, let's start with that Hank Williams tune, *Jambalaya*," Theresa said. "It's a good foot-stomping, hand-clapping song." Theresa started them off with her banjo, then Sarah joined with the guitar, along with Michele on bass. Rachel voiced the verse and they all sang in harmony on the chorus. Then Rachel took over the sound with her fiddle break. Kat on the squeezebox harmonized her voice with Sarah and Theresa as they practiced their patter to lead the audience in the choruses.

Goodbye Joe, me gotta go down the Bayou
Me gotta go, pool the pirogue down the Bayou

It was a great song to start the set because the audience knew it well and they always sang along. Sarah primarily played rhythm guitar with this song, but it was her vocals that sang the lead.

Even though she felt the vibe with the other gals, the blend didn't sound quite right to her, but she couldn't pinpoint the problem. "Could you turn the monitor for my guitar up a little?" Sarah asked after they'd finished. "Also the middle tones in my voice mike seem muddy."

"My voice middle tones have the same problem," Michele echoed.

"Everything's fine for me," Kat said.

"Same here," from Theresa.

Rachel played the fiddle lead break again. "Can you hear that vibration?" She asked. "Not sure if it's the speaker or the mike."

Sarah plucked a few more notes on the guitar and then nodded that she was ready for the next song.

The next song was their usual children's favorite, *A Froggie Went a Courtin'*. The kids always had fun with the *Uh-uh, Uh-uh* refrains. Kat especially went wild on this one, doing knee bends while playing her accordion.

They worked their way through the set from children's songs to a bit of Irish and Scottish ballads led by Rachel. By then Sarah felt she was finally back in the groove. The band was tight. This was familiar territory for all of them. Rachel provided some lighting ideas to Randy, and they tried that again with a couple of the ballads. It really did help set the mood.

By the time they got to Michele's song, *Love's Acceptance*, about her and David's relationship, Sarah was hearing it anew and with more understanding than the hundreds of times they'd sung it before. She remembered with pain how much she'd judged Michele and David's relationship from the very start. First she didn't understand how Michele and David fell into bed so easily after only a few weeks together. Then when it seemed their relationship was going well, David made a mistake and there was no way Michele would forgive him. It was painful to watch.

Just another example of Sarah judging her perception of morality instead of being the best friend she could be to Michele. She hoped she was getting better at letting go of that self-righteous nature now. Especially now that she realized she'd done something similar to Tom when she'd first arrived home.

It was almost as if this song could reflect her own relationship. Love was not easy at all. Nothing like the easy, twinkling starlight, rainbows in romance pictures. You always knew the kiss was perfect because the woman's leg kicked up in the back—as if the kiss went from her mouth all the way to her toes. Love was messy, and trying, and … amazingly more wonderful than she'd imagined.

The second set began again with some uptempo tunes to get the audience re-engaged after intermission. They finished with *Coming Home*, and again the words were more meaningful to Sarah than they'd ever been before. She'd always liked Billy Gilman's lyrics, and today she sang them in harmony with Michele and Theresa with a real feeling for what it was like to come home and to see the world through someone else's eyes.

"Good rehearsal," Randy called from the booth. "I think I have all the lighting cues and the different mixes for both sets. You can leave everything here. I'll make sure it's all locked up."

"Same time tomorrow afternoon?" Kat asked, looking around the group.

Theresa nodded. "Yes. Then Friday is the first show. 5:30 call, 7:00 start."

"I'm turning in," Sarah said. "I'm beat after flying in earlier today."

Rachel tapped her shoulder lightly. "We didn't get to talk about your original song. Kat said you finished it."

"Right," Theresa turned toward her. "We can work it in to the set for Memorial Day weekend if you want to try it and see how people like it."

Sarah rubbed her forehead; she could feel a headache coming on. She had to get some sleep. "Um…the one I finished, I'm not sure I'm ready to bring that in yet. It's more of a plaintive, questioning song."

"That's okay," Kat said. "I like those kind."

Sarah shook her head. "Let me think on it. I have the beginnings of something better in my head already. I just haven't written anything down."

"A love song?" Kat practically danced with the question. "A love song about Tom?"

Sarah couldn't help but smile at her enthusiasm. "Maybe. Now I have to get some sleep." She turned and held her fingers in the air in a little wave as she walked away.

She could barely hear Kat say to the rest of them. "I'll bet I know why she didn't get any sleep."

"Tom." Rachel and Michele said at the same time, and they all laughed together.

She smiled all the way to her hotel room door. She did actually sleep with him last night. Just not in the way they all thought.

"HELLO," Sarah answered her cell phone with a sleepy voice.

"Good morning, sunshine. It's almost noon. I miss you."

She smiled for a moment wondering if she was dreaming of Tom calling her on the phone.

"Sarah? You awake?"

She startled to full consciousness and dropped the phone. She rooted through the blankets and found it again. "Oh, sorry. You're real."

He chuckled. "I like to think so. Dreaming of me?"

"Oh dear." She realized she was sleeping in only underwear and a T-shirt. She fumbled one arm into her robe with one hand while holding the phone with the other. "Just a minute." She put the phone back on the bed and barely managed to get the other arm in before she sat down.

"What's going on there?" He asked. "Sounds like you're dancing."

"Had to get my robe on."

"So I wouldn't see you naked?"

She flushed. "No." The word was drawn out in denial. Yes, that was exactly what she'd been thinking. What an idiot. Of course he couldn't see her.

He laughed even harder. "So you found my secret video camera placed on the ceiling above your bed."

She quickly looked up and then mentally kicked herself for being so gullible. "Ha, ha. Very funny."

"Are you awake now?" he asked. "I want to hear how the rehearsal went, if you are feeling good about being back, if you are excited about the gig."

"So you want to know everything," she said with a smile.

She looked at the bedside clock. It really was noon! She'd slept for fourteen hours straight. She should probably feel guilty, but she didn't. Instead, she snuggled into the pillows; happy to pretend she and Tom were sitting side by side talking as if she'd never left Broken Bow.

She told him about getting to Branson, how fancy the rooms were, how big the venue was, how she was simultaneously excited and scared to play there, and how she wished he was there to share it all with her.

"I might be able to make it for Memorial weekend."

"Really?" Her heart fluttered with delight. That was only two and a half weeks away. "Can you really leave the farm for that long?"

"It depends. I might have some good news by then. I think we have a buyer."

"Already? That's amazing. Is it someone local or an out of town gentleman farmer?"

He cleared his throat. "It's local. Henry Davidson."

"Davidson? Why do I know that name? I can't picture him."

He sighed. "It's Amanda's married name."

Sarah gripped the phone tighter. "Amanda?" She tamped down hard on the automatic angry jealousy from the past. "I can't imagine her on a farm. I've never seen her even in tennis shoes."

"Evidently, they are getting divorced," Tom said, his voice low as if he was consciously trying to keep her calm. "Amanda skipped town and left Henry with the kids. He's always wanted a farm, but Amanda never did. He thinks it will be perfect for him and the kids."

"She just up and left?" Sarah's heart went out to those children. She knew what it was like to lose a mother when you were so young. She didn't really know Henry. She hoped he was a good father. "Is she planning to come back?"

"No one knows. But Henry said he wouldn't take her back even if she did. The rumor is she's been having affairs all over town."

Sarah's voice caught in her throat. She remembered how sure Amanda had been that Tom would be available. She couldn't help but wonder. Amanda was beautiful, and sexy, and … really, what normal single guy would turn her down. What if she planned to divorce Henry so Tom wouldn't have an excuse to not be with her.

"Sarah?" Tom asked after a long pause. "I can tell what you're thinking, and the answer is still no. I have not heard from her. I hope I never do. I have zero interest in ever seeing Amanda again. You are the only one for me."

"I believe you," she answered automatically. She did. What God has joined together let no man, *or woman*, put asunder. No matter Amanda's intentions she trusted that Tom would not fail.

"So, what's Henry's offer," she asked. "Did you accept?"

"I wanted to talk to you first. We set the price at $480,000 and he's offered $375,000. He says that is the value for the land and he doesn't think the house is worth that much."

"We spent a lot of time fixing that house up to sell," Sarah countered. "Or should I say you spent a lot of time. I just did some cosmetic stuff after Dad died." She swallowed for a moment as the death hit her again. It was getting easier not to tear up, but everything was tied up in so many memories. "If he's going to live in it, it can't be all that bad."

"I agree. I think he's right about the land value though. $375,000 for twenty acres seems to be the going rate. The question is if the house is worth another $100,000."

Sarah sighed. "I don't know Oklahoma prices, or even country prices really. It's got to be worth at least fifty though, don't you think?"

"How about if we counter at $450,000?" Tom suggested. "And set our base at about $430,000."

At this point Sarah just wanted to get rid of it and get on with her life. She just couldn't help but also want a fair deal. She also wanted to figure out what was in store for her and Tom. Until the farm was sold he was tied to it, which also meant Tom was tied to Broken Bow.

"Okay," she finally said. "That sounds fair."

"Good, I'll let Scott know the deal, but tell him to negotiate like hell to get us the best he can."

"Thanks," Sarah said. "I don't know what I'd do without your help."

"If this goes through, I'll be up Memorial weekend to see you. You know I've never heard you sing. I remember you noodling with a guitar when we were in high school, but I didn't even know you sang."

"I'm working on a new song," she said. "Actually it's about us. I wasn't sure I'd have it ready in time for the Memorial Day shows, but you've motivated me to try."

"Hmm. So you're going to reveal our passionate love life for all to know?"

"No." Her cheeks warmed. "It's about love and forgiveness." She'd never thought about how he might react. "You don't mind do you? I mean I wouldn't necessarily say this is about me and Tom to the audience."

He chuckled. "I'd be honored that you wrote a song about us and I don't care if the whole world knows." Then he started to sing Paul McCartney's *Silly Love Song* lyrics.

"I'm no Paul McCartney," she said. "Just forget it."

"Come on. Sing me a line or two."

Now she had second thoughts about the whole thing. She wasn't ready to sing it, especially to him.

"It's more about me, I guess, than you." She fingered the blanket.

"What are the first two words?" he tried again.

"We found. That's all you get."

"We found love in the morning, love in the evening, love every time of day," he sang with a country twang. "We found love on Monday, love on Tuesday, love in every way."

Sarah giggled. "Okay, I'll see if I can work in your lyrics."

"Right, I bet you will."

"I'll sing the song when you get here," she said. "If I'm ready, that is. It still needs work."

"Can I motivate you to do something else while I'm there?" He asked, his voice a sexy invitation.

She giggled. "Long walks in the garden? More kisses?"

"Mm hmmm. And ..." he intimated.

"And you'll get to meet the rest of the band."

He laughed. "You are so good. I admire you for that, you know."

"Really? 'Cause I don't think most people understand."

"It means that when we get married, when we make love, it will be like nothing anyone has experienced before. It will be blessed," he said.

Warmth spread over her. He said when we get married. He believed that waiting would make their union blessed. She knew he wasn't a church-goer, though he participated in every part of her father's memorial service. She'd never thought she could marry a non-believer, but now she knew she could.

His heart was good. He followed the golden rule. He led a life of giving, taking care of others, and doing the right thing. She would pray that his heart would open to God's love. She would love to share that part of their journey together. But whether it did or not, she still loved him and would marry him. She'd put her trust in the Lord to see to the rest. There was still a lot to work out...like where they would live, what kind of work he would fine, how they'd manage a relation-ship with her on the road at least half of the year. But she had faith. Faith in Tom. Faith in herself. And above all faith that God had already blessed this union.

"I love you," she whispered, saying it aloud for the first time. "I can't wait to see you again."

Tom's intake of breath was audible.

She waited for him to say something. Certainly her declaration wasn't a surprise. At the airport, she'd laid it all out responding to his kiss.

"Thank you for loving me," Tom finally said. "I never thought I'd have a second chance with you. I wasn't sure how you felt."

"Really?" she asked. "It wasn't obvious?"

"Our attraction was obvious."

She giggled. "Obviously."

"But I wasn't sure you could really forgive our past," he continued. "I believed…hoped…you would learn to love me again, but I wasn't sure."

She grew serious. Sarah didn't want him to doubt her love. She didn't want to ever lose him again. "I do love you, Tom Pawlak. The truth is I never stopped loving you. I hated what you did, but I still loved the man I knew you could be. I think I was looking for that man in every person I dated."

"And now?"

"You are that man and so much more than I ever imagined. You are a good man. A man I can trust. A man I count on to be there no matter the challenges. I feel blessed that I had a second chance, and it has turned out even better than I ever dreamed."

"I will never leave you again, Sarah, no matter what happens in our lives. I will always be there for you."

When they hung up, she wrapped their conversation around her like a blanket. She sat on the edge of her bed with the guitar and the words and music poured out of her. After working through a couple of the lead melodies, she took out a new sheet of paper and wrote it down. This new song reflected coming through the darkness into the light—it reflected hope and love. It reflected the journey she and Tom had made together.

We found love in a heartless place
A place of remorse with no grace
We found love among all the wrongs
To forgive was what we both longed

You said love is not to be earned,
It's a gift with hopes of return.
A fortune that never is spent.
A tree that thrives even when bent.

Chorus:
Alone the rain blinded me.
The fog became my shroud.
But your love helped me to see
the rainbows in my clouds.
Colors flowed in harmony
when our hearts spoke unbowed.
And your love helped me to see
the rainbows in my clouds.

We found love in a heartless place
A place of remorse with no grace
We found love among all the wrongs
To forgive was what we both longed

If darkness makes our love unclear
I'll take your hand and have no fear
As sure as seasons always turn
Our love will forever burn

Chorus (2 times)
Alone the rain blinded me.
The fog became my shroud.
But your love helped me to see
the rainbows in my clouds.
Colors flowed in harmony
when our hearts spoke unbowed.
And your love helped me to see
the rainbows in my clouds.

~

SARAH AWOKE from a deep sleep and turned toward the sound of the phone ringing. The clock registered two in the morning. She sat up straight, afraid that something had happened on the farm. Was Tom hurt? She fumbled in the dark to get to her cell phone and answer.

"Tom? What's happened is everything alright?"

A woman's cackle greeted her. "Tom's great. So sexy. So fine. I'm so glad you had the sense to leave him to me."

She recognized Amanda's voice immediately. She knew there was no way Tom would be with her voluntarily.

"Let me speak with him," she insisted.

"She want's to speak to you darling."

Sarah heard a man growl, but she couldn't tell if it was Tom or not.

"Now." The male voice insisted.

"Come here baby."

Sarah heard something like bed springs squeak as a heavy weight moved.

"Oh, that feel's so good," Amanda breathed into the phone. "Mmmm, yes use your mouth there. Oh. Oh my. Your tongue is amazing," she panted into the phone.

Then Sarah heard a male voice mumble as if he was speaking through a pillow. "No one is better than you." Again she couldn't distinguish if it was Tom.

"I know, babe, no virgin would offer you this."

"Knees," the male said.

"Oh yes. Again. Yes. Yes. Again," Amanda panted into the phone.

Then Sarah only heard heavy breathing and moaning. Then a sound as if something dropped to the floor. The voices were now further away.

"I dropped the phone. Oh, you are bigger than I remembered."

A mans chuckle in the distance and another growl.

"Yes darling, right there. Yes. I know you want it. Take it all. I've been waiting so long."

Amanda's gasp. More breathiness and moans. The sound of a bed creaking.

"Oh you're so big, Tom. I want it. Yes. Now!" Then a slap against a wall or door. "Now. Take me fast and hard, Tom. Yes! Yes!"

Sarah hung up the phone. She refused to believe it. She didn't know how Amanda got her cell number. She was sure that whoever was in the room with Amanda was not Tom. Even if Amanda had somehow forced him into this sick game, Tom would never agree to have Sarah listen in. Why did Amanda want to get back at her so much? She'd already ruined seven years of Sarah's life. There was no way she was going to ruin what she and Tom had now.

Even with those assurances solid in her mind, Sarah's heart raced with anxiety. Was Amanda desperate enough to do something to Tom, like kidnap him? Could she really force him to have sex with her?

Tom had said when Amanda left Broken Bow, no one could find her, not that they tried too hard. Even her husband didn't want to try to find her. Certainly, she wouldn't do anything that would jeopardize her location. With all the men she'd been with, there was no reason for her to focus on Tom. Was there?

She looked at the clock again, and shook her head. She was not going to call Tom at two in the morning and wake him with this. She could talk to him tomorrow. There was nothing she could tonight anyway.

Sarah slipped off the bed and got on her knees, her head cradled on the mattress edge and her hands grasped tightly in prayer. She tried to slow her heart and put the images aside that Amanda had left in her mind. She concentrated on opening her heart to only what was holy.

Lord, protect Tom from whatever is going on. I trust him and I know what just happened does not involve him. But I do not trust Amanda. I ask that you keep him safe and watch over him tonight. Envelop him with your love and your protection.

She stayed there in prayer until she could kneel no more. Exhausted she climbed back into bed and fell asleep.

CHAPTER 13

Tom surveyed the farm with pride. The house looked better than ever. The fields were all planted and the spring growing season looked good. Even though he didn't want to be a farmer for the rest of his life, he would miss this place. He'd found more than a surrogate family here. He'd found himself—the man he'd always wanted to be but didn't think he could become.

He lifted his overnight bag into the trunk and then checked, once again, that he had the final closing papers safely tucked in the front pocket of his bag. When he arrived in Branson, he and Sarah were going to celebrate closing this chapter of their lives. Henry Davidson had accepted the counter at $450,000. They didn't even have to negotiate further.

Tom looked to the tire swing still hanging from the oak tree on the side of the house. He was happy the farm would have children here again. He knew it wasn't going to be an easy existence for Henry and the kids.

Outside of that one horrifying phone call to Sarah, Amanda had not been heard from again. When he'd heard about that call, he'd wanted to fly to Branson immediately and hold Sarah tight to assure her he hadn't strayed. But she'd never questioned his loyalty this time, even after Amanda's try to separate them. Sarah had been calling to make sure he was safe. Her complete belief and trust him helped him to stay and finish up everything with the house and prepare it for Henry and the kids to have a good home when they arrived.

It had been a month, and not a single lead had materialized as to where Amanda ran or what she was doing. Tom shook his head at how prescient he had been, even at eighteen, to cut her loose and not to ever let her in again.

Henry was a good man, a solid, hard-working man who loved his kids. He'd do his very best to raise those boys right. And, if there was any fairness in the world, Henry would one day find himself a good woman too. He deserved a woman who worked just as hard as Henry and would love him and those kids through good times and bad.

He bent to pet Kip, wagging his tail at the truck. "I'll miss you boy. But you'll be happier here with Henry and the boys. They have lots of energy and they need a good companion. They need someone to talk to about everything that's going on."

He opened the passenger door and Kip jumped in ready for a trip, like he'd always done. Tom swallowed hard. "Not today boy. It's going to be a long drive today." He carefully took Kip from the car and placed him on the ground. Then he threw his suitcase on the floor and a light satchel on the seat.

"Go on," he said. "The Davidson's will be here in a couple hours. Go on." He pointed toward the front porch of the house. Kip barked once, wagged his tail, and then turned and raced back to the porch. He made three circles on the porch and then sat, looking toward Tom, his tail wagging.

Tom rounded the truck and slid into the drivers' seat. He took one last look at the farm as he drove out the driveway for the last time.

He didn't look back. His past was finally behind him. As Broken Bow disappeared in his rear view mirror he smiled. Tom was driving toward a great future. A future with Sarah, wherever it might take them.

～

SARAH PACED BACK STAGE. It was the final night of their six- week gig. She'd been singing her new song every night since Memorial Day, and every night Tom loved it even more. After the first night together in her room, they both decided that six weeks of that much togetherness would definitely not leave her a virgin. No matter how committed they both were, she wasn't going to tempt fate every night. She used some of the money from the house sale to get Tom a room just three doors down the hall. Close enough that they could spend every moment together when she wasn't on stage, except for him sleeping overnight.

Everyone in the band had teased her endlessly about the arrangements. It was all good-natured banter, and it would be so easy to give in, but she stood firm. After one more night, they'd all be heading home to Portland. Then she had another bridge to cross. Tom would be staying at her apartment. It was two bedrooms, so they could make some arrangement.

Of course, his solution was to get married immediately. But Sarah wanted to first make sure that Tom loved Portland as much as she did —that he would feel comfortable living there. Portland was very different from Broken Bow. It was a big city, and it had both big-city opportunities and big-city problems. She wanted to make sure he could find his own niche—be his own man.

The band traveled more and more every year, and he wouldn't always be able to go with her. She worried about him coming to Portland with her and then realizing, in two or three years time, that he couldn't live with all the rain or that he would never fit in, that he'd made a mistake in tying his future so close to hers.

"On in ten," Randy interrupted her thoughts.

She shook her head to focus on this last night in Branson. She just had thirty more songs to get through, fifteen in each set. Then the next part of her life would start. She was ready, but was he?

Tom waited in the wings as the band announced their final song and said their goodbyes to Branson. He couldn't take his eyes off Sarah. She sat on a high stool as she played her guitar, one foot propped on the first ring. Her long hair tucked behind her ear and cascaded down her back. He looked toward the audience. Everyone was smiling, having a good time.

The past six weeks had been heaven for him. Mostly heaven anyway. He loved talking with her, dining with her, listening to her practice, and becoming a part of her musical world. He was ready to be married tomorrow, but she still balked at moving so quickly. He still didn't understand why she was afraid to get married. Perhaps she wanted him to get a job.

He'd spent a lot of time with David over the past six weeks. When he and Michele got married, David became the official manager of the band. He'd taken over the marketing, scheduling the tours, and managed all the money. Now with two children and the band becoming even more popular, David was becoming overwhelmed.

Tom had looked at several opportunities to put his business and marketing skills to the test in Portland. After talking to David, he realized that he could put his skills to use for Sweetwater Canyon. It was the best of all possible opportunities. He'd get to do what he loved—PR and marketing—and it would free David up to do pure management on the album and partnership side of the business. All Tom needed was approval from Sweetwater Canyon to seal the deal.

Tom heard loud clapping and feet stomping. He looked up as Sweetwater Canyon bowed to the audience.

Sarah ran toward him and hugged him tight around the waist. Her eyes bright and wide, she looked up at him with a huge smile. "It's over. They loved us. Tomorrow we get to go home."

The stomping and clapping got louder.

"It's a standing ovation," Kat said. "We better get back out with our encore songs."

Sarah laughed and hugged Tom again. "Okay, three more songs, then we can celebrate." She lifted to her toes and drew his face down toward hers. A quick brush of her lips on his and then she turned and walked back on stage with the rest of the band.

Home. Tom rolled the sound of that around in his mind. He'd never been to Portland, Oregon before. He had no idea what it would be like. He trusted that with Sarah it would be wonderful.

The music ended once more and the band walked off the stage for the last time.

"It was good, but I'll be happy to get home," Kat said as they all waited in the wings until the auditorium cleared.

"I'll just be happy to sleep in my own bed, cook my own meals, not have to get up every night and play," Michele said.

"It's been a long tour," Theresa agreed. "And we go out again in three weeks."

Rachel and Michele groaned.

"But it's all in the Pacific Northwest," Kat said. "The folk festival in Sisters, a couple of gigs in Coeur d' Lane, and then I think Vancouver, B.C. and Seattle. Then we get a month break until fall."

"And you go back to school," Theresa added.

"Right. Proms, boys, college visits, boys…" Kat could barely hold back the smirk as Theresa swatted at her shoulder.

Sarah laughed and headed back toward the stage. "Let's pack up, go eat, and celebrate," she said over her shoulder.

Kat ran after her. "Food. Now that's a great idea."

"To the most luxurious six-week gig we've ever had." Theresa raised her glass and everyone followed suit.

"It is nice to have hotel rooms instead of sleeping in Annabelle," Sarah said. "But six weeks in one spot is a little long."

"Agreed," Rachel said, as she leaned into Noel. "But I enjoyed the king sized bed and having a suite where Claire could be close but not too close."

Noel chuckled and pulled Rachel closer.

"What do you mean too close?" Claire asked. "All I have to do is open the door."

"Exactly!" Michele smiled at David as he arranged thinly sliced apples and some chopped orange segments on Tamara's highchair tray. "It was a brilliant idea to get an adjoining kids suite between Rachel and us."

Claire set a piece of orange in front of Tamara and laughed as she held it then threw it on the floor. "I liked sharing a room with Tamara." She picked up the orange piece and put it on a napkin on the table. "But she's a messy eater."

Sarah watched Tamara next carefully nibble on a bit of apple. She sighed and snuggled closer to Tom. For the first time she actually believed she might be a mother one day.

Conversations all started happening at once—reviewing the past six weeks, talking about logistics for the Pacific Northwest tour, and the couples putting their heads together over calendar apps to determine how they would make time for each other.

In the middle of it all, David leaned toward a water glass and struck it lightly with a spoon. The table quieted.

"I have an announcement that needs a vote of all the Sweetwater Canyon members," he said. "Tom Pawlak and I have been talking about the future of PR and marketing for the band."

"Are you giving up on us already?" Rachel teased. "It's only been a little over two years. Have we run you into the ground?"

David smiled. "As you all know I have another business I run as well, and just before this tour Michele and I talked about having another child and what that would do to our already crazy schedule."

"Are you preggers again?" Kat piped up.

"No. Not yet," Michele answered. "But we do want to slow down a bit and enjoy being parents. Tamara's almost two and we wanted the children to be close together enough to be friends."

"Please tell me you're not planning on leaving," Theresa said. "Finding another bass player would not be easy."

"No, not leaving, just thinking about fewer concerts but larger venues," David said. "And that brings me to Tom."

Rachel leaned toward Tom. "Better be careful what you wish for Tom. We are a rowdy bunch of moody, creative women."

"Speak for yourself, Rachel." Sarah said. "Besides, after what Tom has seen me go through I think he could handle one of your tempers with ease."

Rachel laughed. "I like this new you, Sarah. Standing up for yourself. Telling it like it is."

"What you may not know," David continued. "Is that Tom Pawlak has a degree in marketing and PR. He's worked in the field and he would love to take over the bookings and touring aspect of the business."

Sarah turned to him. "Really, you want to be tied to the band? But how can you know you'll even like us? What do you know about musicians and bookings and how crazy picky we can be."

"I've seen a good amount in my two weeks here with you all, and David has filled me in on the good and the bad." He paused. "Scared of having me in your business?" he asked with a teasing note in his voice.

"No. I mean, kind of. Um…of course I want you with me…us…as much as possible. But…oh gosh…I'm making a mess of it aren't I?"

"Yup." Kat said. "Just kiss the guy and say thank you."

"I vote yes," Michele said.

"Me too," Kat said.

"He seems to have the goods for the job," Theresa said. "I vote yes."

"I vote yes, but only under one condition," Rachel said.

Sarah rolled her eyes. She was sure it would be something embarrassing.

Tom smiled. "What is that condition, Rachel?"

"Actually two conditions. First you have to do what Kat said. Kiss her. And not just a little brush across the lips. I mean a real kiss."

Tom pulled Sarah into his arms and lowered his lips. He began with an invitation, which Sarah accepted without thought. Then he moved across her lips with purpose, with promise, and she responded with all the love and hope she wanted to share.

"Wow," Claire said when they finally came up for air. "You kiss better than mommy and daddy. How can you breathe?"

Everyone laughed.

"And the second condition?" Tom asked.

"Please promise me she won't be a virgin within a year. I don't think I can take it anymore."

Everyone laughed a little uneasily.

"That's not fair to ask," Theresa finally said. "Deciding on marriage is something that takes time."

Tom looked Sarah squarely in the eyes. "That's completely up to you. You know I'm ready to marry you any day, any time you say."

Sarah felt her cheeks warm. There was no doubt she wanted to be married to Tom. There was no doubt she wanted to make love to him. She just wanted to know for sure he would be happy. She wanted to know for sure it would all work out.

She scanned each face around the table. They were all waiting with anticipation. They'd easily accepted Tom into their lives. They had nothing but good things to say about him and seemed genuinely happy they'd found each other again.

Tom had told her nothing would be perfect, that they would have to go on this journey together through the challenges and the triumphs. He'd been ready to marry her before she came to Branson, and again when he first arrived. But she was the one who hadn't been ready. She loved him. She wanted to be with him. But she only wanted to be with him if she knew for sure he would be happy in Portland. Now, with a job, one of the two criteria was met.

"Okay, it was unfair," Rachel relented. "I'm sorry, Sarah, I shouldn't have put you on the spot. My vote is Yes to Tom becoming the new marketing guy whether you get married in a year or not."

Everyone clapped.

"Welcome to the Sweetwater Canyon family." Theresa extended her hand across the table to Tom.

Others followed with their congratulations, pats on the back.

"Wait," Sarah said, a little louder than she planned. "I haven't voted yet."

Everyone went silent.

"Oh no," Kat whispered. "Don't blow it, Sarah. Don't blow it."

Tom's eyes widened and one brow quirked up in question.

She took a deep breath and let it out slowly, her heart rate accelerating in anticipation. "I vote yes…on one condition."

Tom nodded and grasped both her hands.

"That we have a Christmas wedding."

"This year?" he asked, his cheeks dimpling as a smile formed. "In about three months?"

She nodded, unable to speak, knowing it meant she was going to trust in an unknown future. She believed in him. She believed in their love. She believed that God meant for them to be together and would help them through the dark times. What better time to celebrate their marriage than during the holidays?

"I accept," he said. "I accept with all my heart." Then he bent and kissed her again. This time with a tenderness that spoke of his steadfast love.

"You had me scared for a moment there at dinner," Tom said, his arm tight around her shoulders as they walked back to their hotel rooms.

"Are you kidding me?" Sarah squeezed his waist. "I had to jump at the chance to have you with me more often. I can't tell you how frustrating it's been when David comes with Michele and they get a room, or Noel comes with Rachel and they get a room. It gets lonely in that motorhome."

"You have Theresa and Kat."

"You know what I mean," Sarah said.

"Ah, so you want us to get a room?" He fished his room key out of his pocket and opened the door. He bowed and gestured for her to enter. "Your room awaits."

Sarah giggled. "Well, not right this minute. You know what I mean."

"Uh huh, I know exactly what you mean." He scooped her up in his arms in one continuous movement, then walked quickly into his room, his foot pushing the door closed behind them.

Sarah giggled again. "You should have saved this part for after we get married."

He lowered her to the floor with a flutter of kisses along her forehead, then each cheek. "I need lots of practice." His voice sounded a little rough. "And when we get married, I'll be undressing you as soon as I close the door."

"Oh." Her eyes widened. She still wasn't used to how easily he talked about his desire for her.

He placed her gently on the bed. His head bent toward her and she opened her mouth slightly, expecting an amazing kiss. He molded his lips to hers, pushed his tongue into her mouth and kissed her until her toes curled.

Then she felt his full weight beside her on the bed. "More practice," he said, his breath shortened. He moved from her lips to the base of her throat, feathering kisses up to her chin and her cheeks, everywhere but her mouth. And she was aching to recapture his mouth.

When he finally returned to her mouth, he was so tender. He stroked his tongue over her lips, gently, softly, sweetly. Wrapping his arms around her, he pulled her body into the curve of his hard chest and kissed her as though she were the most cherished woman on earth, and as if her mouth and her tongue were the only sustenance he craved.

Her body melted and she could do nothing except kiss him back, aching to remove the separation of clothing between them.

He slowly withdrew his mouth and gently held her head to his chest. She could feel the quick, strong beat of his heart, and the deep breaths he was taking to slow it.

"Oh God. Sarah," he gasped out her name. He hugged her even tighter. "I…"

She worked to steady her own breathing. For the past two weeks, every night had been a struggle not to make love. Why didn't she agree to marriage before they left Broken Bow? Why did she keep insisting on torturing both of them this way? It was lunacy. Certainly God knew she was human. After all, they were getting married in just a little over three months. Really, did a month or two head start in bed really matter in the grand scheme of things?

"Tom, I've been thinking…"

His cell phone rang insistently.

He glanced over at it and frowned. "Hold that thought."

He answered the ringing cell phone. "Hello."

"Yes, this is Tom Pawlak."

He sat straight up on the bed. "Oh my God. When? How? What about the children?"

"Thank God."

"No, I have no idea where she is."

"Yes, of course. I'll take the first flight I can get."

He ended the call and stared straight ahead, his hand still gripping the phone tightly.

Sarah gently took it from him and placed it on the night stand. "Tom?" She knelt in front of him, afraid of the far away stare that didn't seem to see her at all. "Tom? What's wrong? What happened?"

"Henry." He continued to stare past her. "Henry Davidson is dead. Shot three times. Direct hits to the heart."

"And the two boys?" She held her breath.

"They're okay. They were asleep. Didn't see anything. Kip woke them with his barking and then…"

She gripped him hard. "They saw? They saw their father dead?"

He nodded. Swallowing multiple times. "Who would do this? Henry had no enemies. Who would leave those boys orphaned?"

"Thank the Lord they weren't killed," she said, rubbing his hands in hers as she quickly offered up a prayer of protection and healing for the boys.

He stood and she followed him. His eyes started to clear, he finally looked at her and gathered her into his embrace.

"I have to fly back tonight."

"Of course," she said automatically.

"When the sheriff arrived on the scene, Henry was holding the guardianship papers. They have no one, Sarah. With Amanda gone, they have no one and Henry had no kin left to take them."

She nodded her head, but couldn't quite take in what this meant. Would this be the end of their relationship? She shook her head vehemently.

"When Amanda left, Henry asked if I would be their legal guardian should anything ever happen to him. At the time I thought it was an easy thing to do to ease his mind. He was in his early thirties and strong and healthy. I never imagined…" He swallowed hard. "I can't let those boys go into the system, not after Henry put his life's savings into your dad's place just for them."

"Of course you have to go," she finally said. "And I'm going with you."

"I can't ask that of you, Sarah. I don't know what's going to happen. I don't know how long it will take. It could be months, or even years." He put his hands on her shoulders and looked directly into her eyes. "I don't know if I have the heart to take them from Broken Bow after all this."

Sarah swallowed back the sob forming in her throat. Just when all her plans were coming to fruition. Just when Tom was finally coming to Portland. It seemed so unfair.

He wrapped his arms around her tighter than she'd ever felt. She could feel his breath next to her ear. "God knows I love you more than life itself," he said into her ear. "But I can't ask you to quit everything again, after you were already away for so long with your father's death. I've seen how important your music is to you. I know that it gives you life."

Now the tears did start to fall. He was right, she couldn't quit her music, but she also didn't want to lose him, again. "What about your new job with the band?" she asked, her voice shaking.

"I don't know," he said. "I don't know anything right now."

"You can work from the farm," she offered. "You're going to need an income."

He said nothing.

"I'm coming with you tonight," she said again.

"Sarah…"

"It wasn't a request, Tom. It was a statement. I'm coming. Yes, my music is very important. But you are the one who fills my life." Her resolve grew firmer, she was going to fight for him, even if it meant they would be apart a lot of the time. "You were there for me and my father, and now I will be there for you. We have a three-week break. That means I have three weeks to help you figure out next steps and get you and the boys settled again."

"Then you'll go back on tour with Sweetwater Canyon as planned?"

She nodded.

She would find a way to balance it all. She didn't have answers right now. But she knew she was not ready to give up either.

"I'll get on the phone and get tickets booked for both of us," she said. "You start packing. I'll call a band meeting in my room, and you can explain as much as possible to everyone."

She turned toward the door. Before she could open it, she felt his body behind her. His arm snaked around her waist and he pulled her tight against him. She closed her eyes and leaned her head back.

Neither spoke. It was as if they silently agreed to simply share this last moment together before the undertow pulled them into the storm. No matter how hard they tried to break with their past, Broken Bow continued to hold them tight in its grasp.

CHAPTER 14

S ARAH AND TOM WALKED INTO THE SHERIFF'S OFFICE hand-in-hand the next afternoon. A man who looked only a little older the Tom stood immediately. At a little over six feet, Tom was of good height. But this man stood at least four to five inches taller.

"Magnus," Tom said, immediately offering his hand to shake.

"Thanks for coming back," the sheriff said. "Those little boys had a rough night. It's only been a couple months since their mom ran out, and now this."

"Happy to help." He turned to Sarah. "Sarah, this is Sheriff Magnus Binford. He came here from Texas about three years ago, and as far as I'm concerned he's the best thing that's happened to Broken Bow policing."

"Well, I don't know about that," Binford said. "I have some good men here."

"Where are the boys?" Sarah asked. "Do they know what happened? Do they understand what's going on?"

"They spent the night at the Roger's farm. You might know it. It's just a mile or so down the road from where your daddy's farm is. The Rogers family is one of two farms in the county licensed as a temporary foster home. She takes kids in emergency situations until they can be assigned a permanent place."

"Do the boys know her?" Sarah asked. "Were they scared?"

"Everyone knows the Rogers family," Tom responded.

"They're good folk. They support the community, the schools, and there's been many times they came out to drop food off for your dad after he took ill."

"Have you interviewed them, Magnus?" Tom asked. "Did they hear anything? See anything?"

"Not that we could tell. It seems they were asleep. According to the coroner, he thinks this happened some time in the early morning. The four-year-old is confused and scared. But I think he hasn't quite grasped that his daddy is never coming home. It's the seven-year-old I'm more concerned about. He definitely knows the situation and he's pretty much stopped talking. He has that dead look in his eyes that I see on people who don't have much hope."

Sarah felt the lump in her throat grow to three times its size. All she could do was squeeze Tom's hand really hard.

"We took Kip out to the Rogers farm too. Connor hasn't let him out of his site."

"What's the situation with the house?" Tom asked.

"Forensics has processed everything. We removed the recliner where he was sitting when he was shot, and several pieces of the wooden floor where he bled out. Those will all be kept as evidence."

"I, uh…have to sit down," Sarah said. Her legs were threatening to give way. She knew he'd been shot, but she didn't really imagine what that meant in terms of the crime scene.

Oh God. Oh God. Oh God. The boys must have found him and called the police. "Those poor boys. I never thought…" She started shaking and her eyes filled with tears at the thought of such a horror visited on young children.

Tom kneeled beside her. "Sarah? Deep breaths."

The sheriff placed a cup of hot tea in front of her. "Take short sips." He rubbed at his chin. "I'm sorry. I shouldn't have been so graphic with my explanation."

She took a sip of the water and then forced herself to sit erect. "It's not your fault," she said. "It just hit me all of a sudden."

"We cleaned up as best we could," the Sheriff said. He turned to Tom. "You'll want to get that flooring replaced and maybe find another chair or something before you move the boys back in there."

Tom nodded. "About that. What is the status of the house now that Henry's gone?"

"Now that's a bit of a conundrum. The house was purchased in both his and his wife's name. But with the wife gone, it's in limbo. You'd have to check with an attorney about next steps. I don't know what the wait time is when someone's just run off and can't be found. Certainly, someone has to pay the mortgage or it will go back to the bank. On the other hand, if we ever find the wife, she would have a right to move back in or sell it or whatever. And if you make payments on the mortgage I don't know what happens there either."

"We'll take it one step at a time," Tom said. "First, we need to get the boys settled again. I assume no one has a problem with us living there at least?"

"No one here in the sheriffs office," Binford said. "My understanding is that the boys, being next of kin, would inherit the house anyway…eventually…if the wife never shows up. Of course, as the legal guardian, you would have use of the house while you raised them."

Sarah shuddered. The thought of Amanda showing back up was another thing she hadn't considered. Was this testing never going to end? *I am not Job* she repeated silently to herself several times. *Lord, please don't give me any more. I can't take it. I've had enough.*

THE FARM HADN'T CHANGED MUCH at all since it sold two months ago. She guessed there was no reason for Mr. Davidson to have made changes. Tom had sown the fields, and they'd spent a good amount of time doing repairs and making sure things were fixed up.

Tom appeared in the window and he opened her door. "You

getting out of the car? Or do you want to stay here until I check things out?"

She forced herself to stand. "I'm coming in with you. We're doing this together. Remember?"

He put his arm around her and drew her close to his side. "Together."

She tucked her arm beneath his and grasped his waist as well. "Let's do it."

As they approached the porch, her dread multiplied. It was as if the house itself didn't want her to ever be happy. When she'd left Broken Bow she'd sworn never to come back. Now she had done it for the second time. Even if she wasn't living here permanently, it felt like she was trapped.

They took the two steps onto the porch together. Then Tom withdrew his arm so he could open the door. The sheriff said the house was unlocked when they arrived. So the first order of business was to put on new locks with keys that only Tom and Sarah had.

He pushed open the door and grasped Sarah's hand. "Ready?"

She nodded, even though the last thing she wanted to do was step inside.

Tom went first and immediately began opening all the curtains in the living room. Sarah followed behind and opened windows to air things out. When she turned to face the kitchen, she saw it—the spot where eight boards or so had been removed from the floor. Even the subfloor there had been removed. When she stood near it, she could see past the floor joists into the basement.

Her stomach clenched. Did that mean the blood wasn't only on the floor, but also seeped into the subfloor? Dear Lord, how much blood had there been? What had those boys seen? The picture in her imagination was bad enough, but seeing in person would be...she couldn't even imagine.

"Why don't you check the barn where we stored extra wood and flooring supplies from when we were fixing the place up to sell?" Tom suggested quietly from only a couple feet away. "I'll check out the rest of the house to make sure nothing else is missing. Then we can make a list and go to town for whatever we need."

Sarah surveyed the living room. There was a sofa along one wall and a coffee table in front of it, but that was it.

"Maybe we could pick up two side chairs from the Salvation Army store. I think we'll want more than that sofa in here," she said.

"Good idea." Tom took a step in front of her. He put his hands gently on her shoulders. "Look at me," he said quietly.

She looked up.

He squeezed her shoulders. "We will get through this. Don't think of the future. Don't think of the past. Just think about today. What we have to do today. That's enough. Then tomorrow we will think about what we have to do that day. And if we keep doing that, things will move along."

"Therefore do not worry about tomorrow, for tomorrow will worry about itself. Each day has enough trouble of its own," she said.

"That's right. You understand then." Tom smiled.

"Not me. Matthew. It's a verse in the Book of Matthew. I used to say it to myself whenever I got nervous about an upcoming gig. Those nerves are nothing compared to this."

She gestured toward the living room. "I just can't get the picture of my mind of those boys finding their father. How horrible it must have been. I don't know what to say to them. I don't know how to act. I'm afraid I'll just start sobbing the minute I lay eyes on them. How their hearts must be broken."

Tom gently placed his hands on each side of her face and tilted her head so he looked directly into her eyes. "I know you, Sarah. You are stronger than you realize. You are the little girl who survived her mother's death. You are the young woman who survived her alcoholic father. You are the woman who can forgive and still love. You are a musician who can bring out emotions in others with your guitar and your lyrics. You are a miracle, Sarah Cosgrave. And, when the time comes for you to say anything to those boys, I know you will put your arms around them and say the exact right thing with the right combination of empathy and we-will-get-past-this-together strength."

He paused and continued to look straight at her, as if he could read every thought, every fear, every insecurity. She wasn't frightened of that thought. In fact, it made her love him all the more.

"Do you believe me, Sarah Cosgrave? Not only can you do this. You will do it brilliantly."

In that moment, she did believe.

TOM PULLED up to the house later that evening with the two boys. Grady was sound asleep. Tom picked up the four-year-old gingerly and cradled him in his arms. Sarah opened the passenger door and loosely offered her hand to Connor. At first he laid his hand in hers but didn't try to hang on tightly. However, as they approached the porch, Connor's little hand gripped hers like a vice. By the time they reached the first stair he stopped and pulled back, his eyes wide.

"What's wrong, Connor?" she asked.

"Is he still in there?" The little boy started to shake.

She stepped in front of him and bent so that her face was level with his. "No, honey. Your daddy is not there. He's in heaven now. Remember, we are going to have a special church service for him next week."

Connor nodded, but his grip did not lessen. "Can he see me from heaven?"

"I believe he can. I believe that he still knows you are here and loves you very much. If he could talk to you he would tell you to be brave and that he is watching you every day."

"Is he like a ghost? Can he touch me?"

"No, he's not like a ghost. Nothing scary."

"Then how does he see me? How can I talk to him?"

"When you and your daddy used to go to church did you ever say prayers? Did you talk to God?"

Connor nodded.

"How do you know that God hears you?"

"Because he's God." Connor said it like everyone knows that's different.

"I think it's because God loves you very much and he wants to hear your prayers. He wants to help you."

A small smile formed just barely lifting Connor's lips at the corner. "And because Daddy loves me very much, he wants to hear me too?"

"That's right!" She tousled his hair. "And you can still talk to him in your heart whenever you like. Even though he might not talk back, just remember that he loves you very much and so he will always try his very best to hear you and to help you."

"That's good," Connor said.

Sarah extended her hand to Connor again. "Are you ready to go in now?"

He placed his hand in hers and together they ascended the steps to the porch.

Sarah held open the door and turned to him. "It's going to look different than the last time you were here. Everything is cleaned up and Tom and I bought two new chairs so everyone has a place to sit in the living room. Okay?"

Connor strained to see around her; then he let go of her hand and dashed into the living room. He stopped in the middle of the room and looked toward the place where the recliner had been. He stood perfectly still, his shoulders tense, raised practically to his ears. His back stiffened, but his legs were flexible, slightly bent as if he was ready to run or pounce. After a few moments, he turned a few degrees to the left and stared again. He slowly scanned every inch of the room as he worked his way turning in a full circle.

Sarah waited by the front door, cringing a little every time Connor turned as he took in a breath. She didn't know what he was looking for, but somehow she knew what he was doing was important to believing he was safe.

When he'd gone full circle and saw Sarah again, he let out a big breath and his shoulders finally came down. "Okay," he said. "It's okay."

Sarah let out a breath of her own she didn't know she'd been holding. Tom was right. Somehow she'd found the right thing to do, the right thing to say.

"He never woke up," Tom said as he re-entered the living room. "I hope he sleeps through the night. Nice bedroom. Well set up for the two boys. Looks like all new stuff."

Sarah glanced around the living and dining room. That was strange considering the rest of the house looked like second-hand furnishings. Not just the two chairs she and Tom bought recently, but everything.

"Mommy bought it for us," Connor said, his eyes downcast as he said it.

Tom and Sarah looked at each other at the same moment, each forming a little "O" with their mouth.

"When did she buy it, Connor?" Sarah asked.

"The day before she went away. She said we needed some things to last because she was going to be gone a long time."

"That was really nice of her," Sarah said as she sat on the sofa. She stared at Tom and tried to gesture for him to follow up. No one had told them Amanda talked to either of the boys before she left. As far as the police knew, she just walked out the door one day and it was a surprise to everybody—especially poor Henry.

Tom sat in the chair nearest the kitchen—not the one they'd placed over the new floor section. "Did your mommy say how long she would be gone?"

Connor canted his head to one side as if trying to remember, then he straightened up. "I promised not to tell anybody."

"Not even your dad?" Sarah asked.

"Mommy said it was a game she and Daddy played, like hide and seek, but it would last a lot longer then one day. And Daddy had to find her, so I couldn't tell him."

"Hmmm. But she's been hiding a long time. Don't you think it's time you told someone?" Tom asked.

"I don't know," Connor said. "You're not supposed to tell secrets to other people."

Sarah searched for a way to let Connor know it was okay to tell without him feeling like he was betraying his mother.

"I think she wouldn't mind if you told us now," Tom said. "It's been a long time. Maybe she got lost and wants us to find her."

Connor shook his head. "No, she's not lost. I know where she is."

"You do?" Sarah asked, trying not to let the excitement of discovery show in her voice. "You've seen her since she ran..I mean, since she started the game of hide and seek?"

Connor nodded. "Uh huh. We have a secret meeting place where she comes once a week to talk to me and see how I'm doing."

"Where is it?" Tom asked, leaning back in the chair like it didn't matter. "I'm not playing the game. I'd like to see her too."

"She said 'specially don't tell Mr. Tom because he would tell Daddy and then she would lose the game."

Tom looked back to Sarah, his brows raised.

"Connor," Sarah tapped the sofa next to her. "Would you please come and sit beside me. I have a problem I need you to help me figure out, and it's easier to talk if you're right here."

Connor looked at her for a minute, but then walked to the sofa and sat on the edge as if ready to run if he changed his mind.

"Grown ups don't have problems. Besides I'm just seven and you're smarter than me."

"Lots of times adults don't know all the answers," Sarah said. "Will you help me?"

He sat up straighter and scooted back toward the other end of the sofa. He faced her and crossed his legs. "I'll try. What is your problem?"

"Do you know who my best friend is?"

Connor looked over at Tom and pointed.

"That's right. And when my daddy was very sick, Mr. Tom helped take care of him. And when I came home to take care of him too I was very sad because I knew he was going to die soon."

Connor frowned and dipped his head. "I remember Mr. Jack. Mommy called him a...um...a corn mud gun. That's right, a corn mud gun. I don't know what that is, but she didn't say it in a mean way or anything."

Sarah smiled. "I think you mean a curmudgeon."

"That's it. You said it right. What is it?"

"It means a person who is set in his ways, stubborn and sometimes hard to get along with."

"Oh. I'm sorry. I guess I shouldn't have said that."

"No, it's fine. My daddy was a curmudgeon, but he loved me and I loved him and that's what really matters doesn't it?"

Connor nodded. "And he died. I remember now. Daddy wanted to go to Mr. Jack's funeral but he and Mommy had a fight so we stayed home instead. Are you sad about your daddy? Is that your problem? I'm sad about my daddy too."

Sarah swallowed. She remembered how no one showed up except Tom and Sweetwater Canyon. It made her like Mr. Henry even more to know that he would have come to pay respects if it weren't for Amanda.

"And your daddy loved you and Grady very much too," Tom picked up the conversation when Sarah couldn't continue. "It's okay to be sad. Both you and Sarah will have some sad times now. But it also helps to think of all the good things your daddy did."

"I remember once when I went down to the river fishing, and I kept moving to find the fish, and I got lost and I was scared and Daddy came and found me. That's a happy and a sad thing. Is that okay? To remember happy and sad together?"

"Yes, any memory is okay if it's the truth," Tom said. "Don't you think he would be worried about you now because he's not here to take care of you and your mommy is not here to take care of you either?"

"But you and Miss Sarah are here," Connor said. "And Miss Sarah said Daddy can see me from heaven, so he knows I'm okay."

Tom gestured toward Sarah and raised his shoulders as if he had no idea where to go now.

"You're right," Sarah said. "He knows that Mr. Tom and I will take care of you no matter what." She searched for a way back to her questions. "Anyway, back to my problem. You see, Mr. Tom is my best friend, but he was also your daddy's friend. Did you know that?"

"Kind of. My Daddy said Mr. Tom was a good man and I could trust him if I was ever lost or needed help and Daddy wasn't there to help me."

"Exactly! And that's why he's taking care of you. Because he knows you need help. But Mr. Tom is also worried about your mommy because nobody knows where she is, and maybe she doesn't know that your daddy's in heaven now and that the hide and seek game is over. Don't you think she would want to know about your daddy and come to the funeral?"

Connor nodded and his eyes misted, but he didn't cry. "I'm worried about her too because I ran to our secret place to find her and tell her to come help Daddy when he was bleeding, but she wasn't there. And I left her a message in the tree to come back and I've checked lots of times and no one has picked up the message and I don't know what to do now."

Sarah scooted closer to Connor. "Oh honey, I'm so sorry. Come here. I need a hug because I'm sad about that. Could you give me a hug?"

Connor scooted closer and leaned into her, wrapping one arm around her waist. She hugged Connor back.

Tom joined them on the sofa on the other side of Connor and scooted in to hug both of them. "I need a hug too," he said. "I think all of us miss your daddy very much."

Then Connor started to cry. At first it was the small, sudden intakes of breath, the hiccuppy types of sobs. But then it grew and grew until he was clinging so hard to Sarah's waist she was sure she might have bruises. But it didn't matter. This little boy had been carrying the burden of the world on his shoulders.

And it made her detest Amanda even more. What kind of woman would be so self-centered as to put such a burden on a seven-year-old?

After several minutes of sobbing and hugging, Connor let go. "I'm sorry Miss Sarah," he said between hiccups and trying to catch his breath again. "I'm not supposed to cry because I have to be the man now."

"Men cry too," Tom said. "Sometimes crying shows how much you care. Sometimes you have to cry because things are so bottled up inside that if you don't, you might explode or get sick."

Connor looked up at him. "Do you cry?"

"Yes, lots more than you'd imagine. I cried when my best friend moved away."

"You mean Miss Sarah?"

Tom nodded and Sarah's heart melted.

"I cried when my mother died, and I cried when Sarah's daddy died."

"Boy you cry a lot," Connor said, through a partially choked voice.

Tom chuckled. "It does sound that way. The point is that when you love someone and that person goes away, it is okay to cry. You have lots of emotions bottled up inside you that need to come out. Your daddy died, and you're scared, and you miss your mommy. Those are all very good reasons to cry."

"And we would really like to help find your mommy and tell her about your daddy," Sarah added. "Don't you think that makes it okay to tell us your secret?"

Connor nodded. "I forgot that Daddy wasn't playing the game anymore." He took a big breath and let it out again. "Mommy said she was hiding out with her friend, Mr. Justin. She said that Daddy would never find her because he doesn't like to golf."

"Justin Winters?" Tom asked. "The man who owns the golf resort?"

"Yeah. Mommy said she gets to stay in a fancy room at the big motel there, and someone else has to clean it and she gets to go swimming whenever she wants and eat whatever she wants and go shopping and stuff like that. Oh, and Mr. Justin gives her presents all the time, and she said that maybe one day he would give me and Grady presents too. But not jewelry like he gives her. That would be stupid. We could get something cool like a video game or something."

"Sounds like a fine time your mom is having," Tom said through gritted teeth.

Sarah hugged Connor again. "Thank you for telling us. Tomorrow Mr. Tom will go out to the resort and see if he can find your mommy. Okay? And he'll tell her about your daddy too."

"Do you think she'll come home then and take care of us?"

"I hope so," Sarah said. "I hope so."

~

AFTER they finally got Connor to sleep in his room, Tom called Magnus and told him everything Connor had said. They agreed that Magnus would drive out to the resort and see if he could locate Amanda.

After the phone call Tom and Sarah sat side by side, on the sofa, wrapped in each other. Neither one spoke, as if putting the situation in words would somehow make everything even uglier than it already was.

Sarah was so filled with anger that she didn't even know where to start the conversation. In fact, she wasn't sure she wanted anyone to find Amanda and bring her home. She obviously didn't care about anyone except herself. The boys deserved better. Henry had deserved better too.

Tom rubbed his hand in circles on Sarah's back. She wondered if he could feel the anger seething through her. For the first time in her life she felt like she wanted to wring another woman's neck.

Sarah tried to slow her breathing. She remembered the verse in Romans 14: *Repay no one evil for evil, but give thought to do what is honorable in the sight of all.* She knew that Amanda would answer for her sins eventually. But trusting that was really hard right now.

Sarah pulled away from Tom and stood. The circles weren't soothing anything. "If Amanda hasn't shown up after everything that happened, I don't think she's coming back."

"She'll be back," Tom said. "Even if I have to throw her over my shoulder and drag her back. She doesn't get to just walk away from her children."

Sarah paced the length of the sofa and back again. "Is it possible something awful happened to her too? I mean, how could any mother leave her own kids like that. I'll bet she and Justin don't even know what's happened. I'll bet they're off on some romantic trip in Bermuda or Jamaica or something. And what about Justin's wife and his kids? Do you think she knows anything?"

Tom shrugged his shoulder. "Justin's always been a player. I think he was messing around within the first month of his marriage. As for his wife, I've never understood why she stays with him. I don't really know her. I occasionally see her in town shopping but that's about it. She's never been one to come to charity events at the golf club or to put herself out there in social situations with Justin."

"I don't blame her," Sarah said, still angry. "Would you if you knew that everyone in town knew your spouse was an adulterer? I wouldn't. In fact I'd move away."

"And you did," Tom said.

She stopped abruptly. "You weren't an adulterer," she said slowly. "Not exactly. We weren't married or anything."

"It was close enough," Tom said. "I knew we had an unspoken agreement of exclusivity. I will never forgive myself for how much I hurt you, Sarah."

"I've forgiven you." She whispered. "I know you're a changed man."

"And I am humbled by your forgiveness," he said.

Then she shook her finger at him. "But if you ever try it again, I'll…I'll cut off your…well I won't really do that but I'll be thinking it. I will definitely be thinking it."

Tom chuckled. "I've been forewarned. If I didn't have enough incentive already, that picture would be scary."

Sarah sat down on the sofa again and leaned into Tom. He put a loose arm over her shoulders. She really did believe he wasn't a womanizer. And now that she knew more about Amanda, she had an idea how Amanda may have lured Tom away and started him down the road of perdition. When Tom ran off with Amanda before, Sarah completely blamed Tom. She never blamed Amanda. Now she wondered.

"I didn't really know Justin in high school," Sarah said. "All I knew is that he was one of the rich kids and out of my league. Who did he marry? Someone we knew?"

"Cindy Lusson?"

"Dear Lord, no wonder she puts up with it." Sarah snuggled further into Tom. "Poor Cindy, the sins of the father…"

"You know her?"

"I know her daddy better. He was a notorious womanizer. He used to drink with my dad and tell tales of all the women he'd bedded. When I'd go to drag Daddy out of The Office bar and bring him home, Mr. Lusson was always there with a bunch of drunk men listening to the story of his latest conquest. I remember thinking he probably had the proverbial notches on his bedpost with initials for each woman. To hear him tell it, nearly every woman in town had been conquered."

She sighed and turned around to look at Tom. "At least that's one thing my Daddy wasn't. He was never an adulterer."

"He was loyal to those he loved," Tom agreed. "That is a lesson he taught me over and over."

He canted sideways on the sofa and pulled Sarah in close, so that her back was snuggled against his chest. She leaned her head back as he wrapped both arms around her waist. It felt so good, so natural to be here with him—to be tackling this problem with Grady and Connor. In some ways, it felt like she imagined they would be together when they had their own children.

He turned her chin slightly up and looked at her. "Sarah? Are we still okay? With the future even more murky then we ever imagined?"

She crawled completely into his lap and hugged him as tears formed in her eyes. Was there ever a best time to say yes? She'd learned that God didn't always present her with the answers she sought at the time she wished. She was scared of being hurt again, even though she trusted Tom. She was scared of being stuck in Broken Bow, even though she knew that she would stay if that was best for those two little boys and that was what Tom needed.

"Yes, we're okay," she said. "I'm scared to death, but I will trust in the Lord to keep us safe and on the right path together."

CHAPTER 15

TOM AND SARAH HURRIED THE BOYS INTO THE CAR. Tom secured the car seat for Grady while she made sure that Connor knew how to use his seat belt correctly. It had been a hectic breakfast. She'd scrambled some eggs while Tom made the bacon and poured milk and orange juice. Then Tom ran morning baths for the kids while she cleaned up the dishes. She had naturally fit into the morning routine with Tom and the boys, and it was only the first day. She smiled as she secured her own belt in the front seat.

"Everybody buckled up and ready to go?" Tom asked.

"Yes!" The two boys immediately answered.

"Okay, now what?"

Connor giggled, "Turn on the car Mr. Tom."

"Oh, that's right. I almost forgot."

Sarah squeezed the top of his leg. He was so good at helping the kids feel at ease. How did she end up so lucky to fall in love with Tom Pawlak?

"Miss Sarah, do you think the sheriff is going to be mad at me for not telling him my secret before when he asked me?" Connor asked from the back seat.

"No. He will be proud of you for being loyal. And he will be very happy you are now helping him to find your mommy."

"Do you think Mommy will be mad at me?"

Sarah hesitated. Amanda probably would be mad if she didn't want to be found. But she wasn't going to say that to Connor.

"If you were playing hide and seek and got lost, would you be mad at the people who tried to find you?"

Connor shook his head. "No. I would be happy they found me."

"I would too," Sarah said. "So, let's just concentrate on finding your mommy, okay?"

Tom pulled into a parking space near the front door of the sheriff's office. "We're here."

"Okay," Connor finally responded as he unbuckled.

A slightly rumpled, grey-haired woman greeted them at the door. She smiled and said, "I'm Mrs. Dale and I'm in charge of taking care of children. So who is named Davidson here?"

Both Connor and Grady said "Me!"

"Well, it happens I have only two suckers; and the sheriff said I can only give them to someone named Davidson. Are you sure that's you?"

Both boys nodded vigorously.

"Okay then, here you go." She fished her fingers into a deep pocket on her jacket and pulled out two round dum-dum pops, one chocolate and one grape. "Who gets what?"

"Purple, purple, purple," Grady shouted.

"I'll take the chocolate, thank you," Connor said.

She handed each to the boys. "Now work on that slowly so it lasts a long time." Then she bent toward Grady to help him unwrap his pop. "Grady, you and I are going to go right over there." She pointed toward an office to one side of the desk. It had a clear glass front and Sarah could see there were some small toys on the table.

Grady looked at Tom and pointed his finger. "You come."

"I need to go with Miss Sarah and Connor first," Tom said. "We need to talk to the sheriff first. But as soon as we're done we will come too."

A small pout formed on Grady's lips. Sarah was afraid he might cry or balk at going anywhere without Tom. "How about if I walk with you over there and let's see what fun we can have?"

She took Grady's hand and walked toward the glass room. Waving her fingers over her shoulder, she caught Tom's mouthed "Thanks" before he and Connor were ushered down the hall into another room to meet with Sheriff Binford.

~

Sheriff Binford held his hand out to Connor. "Thanks for coming in, son."

Connor shook his hand. "You're welcome, sir."

The Sheriff gestured to the two chairs in front of his desk. "Have a seat. You too, Tom."

"I'm not going to jail, am I?" Connor asked.

"No. No. No. We don't put little boys in jail. Why do you think you should be in jail?"

"I don't. I was just afraid, you know, because I lied to you before. You know, about my mom."

"Well, that is true." Binford tapped his pen on a tablet of yellow paper. "Mr. Tom told me that you were only doing what your mom told you, so I can't get you into trouble for that. Right? Your 'sposed to do what your parents say."

"I...I guess so."

"In the future though you need to understand that I'm your friend too. And sometimes I have to ask questions that even adults don't like. And most of the times that means people have to tell me their secrets, even when someone else said not to. But it's never wrong to tell a policeman."

"Why? You're someone and Mommy said not to tell anyone. Not even Grady and 'specially not Mr. Tom."

"Sometimes adults ask you to keep secrets without realizing that doing that can hurt people—even the people they love the most. When somebody dies, my job is to find out all the secrets of everybody who knew that person. Because one of those secrets will help us solve a big puzzle. The problem is I don't know which one will be the most helpful until I hear them all. It's like a big jigsaw puzzle of secrets."

"You mean my secret may help find my daddy's killer?" Connor grasped the arms of the chair hard.

"That's right."

"Then I'll tell you everything. Anything you want. I'll even tell you about the time I got mad and ran away from home and didn't tell anybody. And when I came back and Daddy asked me where I'd been, I lied and told him I was at a friend's house. But really I was running away."

Tom barely held back a chuckle.

Sheriff Binford smiled. "That's a pretty big secret, son. But I don't think I need to know that one. You can keep that one to yourself."

"Oh." Connor scooted back in the chair. "I guess you and Mr. Tom know it now though."

The sheriff leaned back in his chair. "How about if I ask the questions, and then you just tell me the truth? Is that okay with you?"

"Sure. That's fine."

He pointed to a machine on his desk. "This is a recording machine. Is it okay if I record this, in case I lose my notes or write something down wrong?"

Connor looked at Tom. "Do you think it's okay, Mr. Tom?"

Tom nodded. "I think it's a good idea."

"Okay then," Connor said.

The Sheriff pushed a button and Tom could hear the click as the recording started. "Sheriff Magnus Binford interview with Connor Davidson. Also in the room is the appointed guardian, Tom Pawlak."

"That's right so far," Connor said.

The sheriff snorted as he tried to hold in laughter. "Um, thanks for verifying that. So, let's start with when your mother decided to leave."

"She didn't leave, sir. She was playing a game with Daddy. Hide and seek."

"Is that so?" He wrote something down on his yellow pad. "When she told you she was playing hide and seek, exactly what did she say to you?"

Tom listened as Connor recounted the same story he'd told him and Sarah last night. It was almost word for word about Amanda's game and about her living at the golf resort with Justin Winters. It was so close to the original telling that Tom was confident it was the truth as Connor understood it. The sheriff took copious notes and often said back exactly what Connor said to verify he'd heard it right.

Connor didn't seem nervous at all once he got past the worry of being in trouble. In fact, it looked like he was proud to be doing something to help find out who killed his father.

"Now this is very important," the Sheriff said. "And it's going to be hard to talk about."

Connor gripped the desk in front of him.

"Take me through what happened the night before your father died."

"You mean, like, after the phone call?"

Tom scooted his chair closer to Connor. "A phone call? I don't think I remember you talking about that before."

"I don't know, I didn't think it mattered because it was before I went to sleep, and Daddy got killed while we were asleep and I didn't see it. Maybe if I had stayed awake instead, I could have saved him." Connor's lip trembled and he swallowed several times.

Tom turned both of their chairs until they were directly facing each other. Then he put his hands on Connor's shoulders. "I want you to listen to me very carefully. Can you do that right now?"

Connor nodded his head, but Tom could tell he was holding back the tears with everything he had.

"It is not your fault that your father died. Even if you were awake there was nothing you could have done to save him. Do you understand?"

"Yes, but—"

"There is no but, Connor. Whoever did this was determined to kill your father and if you had been there, you and Grady may have been killed too. Maybe the killer didn't even know you were there and that saved you."

"Are…are you sure?"

"I'm very sure."

"I'm sure too," the sheriff said.

Connor sat staring straight ahead. "The person who did this is really bad," he said, his voice barely a murmur.

"The worst," Sheriff Binford said.

Connor took a deep breath and turned back to the sheriff. "I want you to catch him. I want you to put him in jail forever. I don't want him to kill anybody else."

"That's exactly what I want too, son."

"This is pretty scary stuff," Tom said. "Remember when we talked about feelings and sometimes men need a hug too?"

Connor nodded.

"Well, I think I need a hug again," Tom said. "How about you?"

Tom opened his arms and Connor climbed into his lap and hung on tight.

After a few minutes he turned around, but he didn't leave Tom's lap. Tom kept an arm around Connor, not too tight but just so he knew it was there.

"Do you have more questions?" Connor finally asked.

"Good boy," Binford said. "Let's go back to that phone call. Do you know what time it was when the phone rang?"

"I think it was a little after nine o'clock because that's my bedtime and I was in bed and Grady was already asleep but I was kind of mad because I didn't want to go to bed yet."

"Good information," the sheriff said. "So, you were wide awake and kind of mad when you hear the phone ring. Is that right?"

"Yeah, I heard the phone ring and my daddy picked it up. I had to open my door a crack so I could hear him talking."

"And then what?" The sheriff asked.

"Daddy was quiet for a long time, and then he said something like 'You can't do that. Don't you care for anybody other than your self.' And then he listened some more. And then he said some swear words

I can't tell you because I'm not allowed to swear. And then he said, 'You're not getting a penny out of me' and he slammed down the phone and stomped into his bedroom."

"Who do you think he was talking to?"

"I don't know, I couldn't hear the other person."

"Did your daddy ever say a name, like when he yelled at that person?"

Connor worried his lip as he thought. "I don't remember a name. Is it real important?"

"Don't worry about it," the Sheriff said. "It might come to you later. So, did your daddy get phone calls very often that made him mad?"

"Um…I don't think so. This is the first time I remember him getting mad at anybody except Mommy. Sometimes he and Mommy would shout at each other."

The sheriff's eyebrows lifted slightly. "Hmmm. What did they usually fight about?"

"I don't know, they always said it was grown-up stuff."

"It probably was grown-up stuff, but sometimes even if you don't understand it can still be important," the Sheriff said.

"Do you remember any of the words they used?" Tom asked.

"One time they were talking about you, Mr. Tom. Mommy said she would go live with you because you had plans, you went to college and stuff. Then Daddy said that you were too smart to let her live with you. And then Mommy said that she knew how to make you change your mind. That she'd done it before and she could do it again. And then they called each other a lot of bad names and Mommy ran out of the house."

Tom didn't know what to say. He could only imagine what really happened during that fight. It definitely sounded like Amanda was planning to leave for greener pastures. She was looking for a sugar daddy. And she probably found one in Justin Winters.

"Mr. Tom is it true you wouldn't let Mommy live with you? If we find Mommy, then can she live with you and me and Grady?"

"Let's get back to the questions, okay Connor?" The sheriff saved Tom from having to answer.

"Oh, sorry. I forgot," Connor apologized.

"When your mommy and daddy had fights did they hit each other?"

"Daddy never hit Mommy, but sometimes Mommy would hit Daddy. He never got hurt bad or anything. It wasn't like a karate fight. It was like she would sock him in the shoulder or slap him in the face."

"And he never hit her back?" The sheriff asked.

"No, and he always told me I should never hit a girl either, even when they're mad."

"When your mommy and daddy had fights, did they call each other names?"

Connor looked down as if he was embarrassed. "Sometimes my Mommy would call Daddy stupid or a bad word I'm not allowed to say."

"It's good that you don't say bad words, but it may be important. Could you whisper them to Mr. Tom?"

Connor whispered into Tom's ear.

"Amanda used the word that ends in hole," Tom said. "And then Henry would use a word that rhymes with witch and then Amanda would leave the house."

"Thank you, Connor. I know it's hard to say those words, even in a whisper. I'm proud that you don't say them normally." He paused. "Now think back to that phone call. When your daddy was getting angry and talking on the phone, did he use any of those words like he did when your mommy and he were fighting at home?"

Connor's eyes widened and he nodded. "The one like witch." Then he started talking very fast. "Do you think he was talking to Mommy on the phone? Do you think she was done with playing hide and seek? Maybe when she heard about Daddy on the news, she ran away 'cause she was scared the killer would come after her too. Do you think the killer knows about me and Grady and he's going to come after us now?"

Tom felt Connor's heart speed up. "I don't think the killer is going after anyone else," he said. "In fact, I think the sheriff already has some ideas about who the killer may be. Isn't that right Sheriff?"

"Yes, you've been very helpful, Connor. You've been very brave. However, just to be safe, I'm going to make sure there is a deputy in front of your house every day until we catch the killer. So, if you ever get scared and you can't find Mr. Tom or Miss Sarah, you can run to that deputy and tell him you're scared okay?"

"Okay."

The sheriff stood. "I think I have everything I need now." He pressed a button on his phone and said, "Mrs. Dale, would you come in here please?"

The kind lady, who had greeted them when they arrived, quickly entered the room.

"Connor would you please go with Mrs. Dale and join Miss Sarah and your brother? I need to talk to Mr. Tom alone for a few minutes."

Connor climbed out of Tom's lap and turned to him. "Are you going to be okay? If you're scared I can stay here and still give you hugs so you won't be scared."

Tom held back a smile. "That's very considerate of you, Connor, but I think I'll be okay. I think all the scary stuff is over now. Isn't that right Sheriff?"

"Yup. No more scary stuff," the sheriff said.

"I'll come join you before you even finish your sucker," Tom said.

"Oh, I forgot about it." Connor pulled it from his jeans pocket. The stem was a little bent but still in one piece. "Okay, it's a deal, but if you get scared you can call me."

"I'll do that," Tom promised.

Mrs. Dale placed a hand gently on Connor's back and ushered him to the door. Tom could hear her asking him about how old he was and where he went to school as they walked down the hall.

The sheriff closed his office door. "That's one amazing young boy," he said. "He's holding up real well considering what he saw and what's happening in his life."

"Are you thinking what I'm thinking?" Tom asked.

"I suspect so. What are you thinking?"

"That Amanda may have something to do with this," Tom said. "Did you send someone out to Winter's place to find her?"

"She wasn't there," Magnus said. "Winters said she took off a couple of days ago and he has no idea where."

"Do you believe him?" Tom asked.

"Doesn't matter if I believe him. Without a warrant to search the resort there is nothing I can do. Right now I can't get a warrant because all I have is suspicions. Do you think Amanda is capable of killing her husband?" the sheriff asked.

Tom took in a breath. "God I hope not. I mean she is self-centered and manipulative, and I definitely think she is with Justin for one reason only—the money. But killing? Why? She has what she wants, no responsibility and lots of money. What motive would she have for killing Henry? He was a good man and he was taking care of the kids."

"Maybe she wanted a divorce and Henry didn't agree," the sheriff suggested. "Or maybe she wanted the kids and Henry wasn't going to give them up. Whatever the reason, I'll bet my last dollar that she's involved."

Tom shook his head. "I can't see her being the killer. I just can't."

"Then maybe she hired someone to do the killing for her," Binford said.

Tom reeled with unanswered questions. He couldn't imagine Amanda hiring someone to kill Henry. What would she gain? She was already having affairs all over town and Henry was working, paying the bills, and taking care of the kids. No, she may be a manipulative social climber, but a killer? He couldn't wrap his brain around that possibility.

"I've got to ask you something else," Binford said. "I know about the relationship you had with Amanda in high school. Since you returned to Broken Bow have you had or do you now have any kind of relationship with Amanda Davidson?"

"No, absolutely not." Tom was firm.

"Then why would she single you out, of all the men in Broken Bow, to warn Connor not to tell you about staying with Winters? And why would she throw your name in the face of her husband when they fought?"

"I don't know," Tom said. "She has come round to see me and fling herself at me from time to time. But I've always turned her down. I've always told her to work things out with Henry."

"But did you make it clear you weren't interested? Or was it that you weren't interested as long as she was married. Is it possible that she killed her husband in order to be freed up to marry you?"

Tom stood. "No! No, no, no." He paced in front of the desk. "Oh my God, is it possible? Was that why she called Sarah in Branson?"

"She called Sarah?" the sheriff asked. "Tell me about it."

Tom reiterated that horrific call. "But she hasn't called since."

"Why would she want to pretend she was with you?" the sheriff asked.

"Because she's crazy?" Tom said. "She's always been jealous of Sarah, even long after Sarah left Broken Bow. Whenever I would turn down her advances, she would make some comment about how I would take her up on it if she looked like or acted like Sarah."

"Sounds like a woman obsessed to me," the sheriff said.

Tom shook his head. "I'm not what she wants. I don't have money. I'm not the type of guy she goes for. Winters is her type. That's why she's with him. I'm just a guy she can't control anymore. That's all. But she doesn't really want me."

"Are you sure?" The Sheriff insisted. "Are you sure she isn't secretly in love with you, even if you couldn't offer her everything she wanted?"

Tom's heart rate sped to double-time fearing the thought of her being some type of crazy stalker woman. "Whatever she feels for me is not love," he said. "I agree there's something wrong with her to keep doing this. I don't know what it is. If it is an obsession, it isn't because of anything I've done. I told her I wasn't interested. And I'm not. She's poison."

Tom sat and put his face in his hands. "Oh my God, do you think Sarah's in danger?"

"It's a possibility," Binford said. "That's one reason I'm assigning someone to watch your house 24/7."

"I couldn't live with myself if something happened to her."

"I think it would be best to send her away," the sheriff said. "If all this is some ploy to be with you, the best thing you can do to keep her safe is get her away from Broken Bow."

"Do you think she'd hurt the boys?" Tom asked.

"If she meant to harm them, it would have happened when Henry was killed."

"And what if it isn't Amanda?" Tom asked. "Who else is on your suspect list?"

"Frankly, you."

"Come on, Magnus. You know me. Besides I have the best alibi, I was three hundred miles away in Branson, Missouri with Sarah and the band when all this happened. I came back when you called me."

"You could have hired someone," the sheriff said. "And it is curious that the one legal document obvious in Henry's house was the guardianship papers. Why would that be, Tom? You said yourself you two weren't particularly close. You'd been gone with Sarah for two weeks, with plans not to come back to Broken Bow and yet Henry died holding these papers. It just doesn't add up."

"I agreed to be the boys guardian after Amanda left him. Henry was a careful man. He didn't expect Amanda ever to come back and he wanted to be sure if anything happened to him the boys would be cared for by someone they knew. He was thinking about a traffic acci-dent or a farm accident. I never thought it would come to this. Henry was strong and young. He was careful and knew what he was doing on the farm. I just agreed to give him a little peace of mind."

"But he was holding that legal document when we found the body. Isn't it odd that in the struggle he had the wherewithal to get to his files and find that piece of paper and grasp it while he bled out?"

Tom threw up his hands. "I don't know, Magnus. I agree it sounds weird. It sounds unbelievable that he could do that after being shot three times in the chest. Maybe I'm being set up. I don't know. I only know I had nothing to do with this."

Magnus ran his hands through his hair and puffed out a frustrated breath. "Everything I know about you is that you are a stand-up guy. That's why I haven't arrested you. But I also know that sometimes stand-up guys do bad things. I'm hoping that's not the case with you, but I'm keeping my options open. All I know right now is this case is tied to you in some way and I want to know why."

Tom shook his head. "I don't have any answers for you."

"Go home, Tom. Talk to Miss Sarah and convince her to leave. Take care of those boys. You're doing right by them. I can see that. We'll talk again in a couple days. We'll see what develops after Miss Sarah leaves."

CHAPTER 16

"No! Absolutely not. I will not leave you here to face this alone. There is nothing you can say to convince me to leave! Nothing!" Sarah crossed her arms and glared at him.

"How dare you even ask. If this has anything to do with Amanda I'm staying here to set her straight. I am not running away this time. We've tackled this whole horrifying event together, and I am not leaving now. Do you hear me? Not! Not! Not!"

Tom sat on the bed unmoving. His plan was to let her have her say and then try again. Sometimes she just needed to let off steam. There was no way he was going to let her stay if there was even a small chance that she'd be in danger.

Sarah paced the floor, her hand clenched and her mouth tight. He hadn't seen her this mad since high school.

"Sarah," he said quietly. "Please, let's talk this through. Even Sheriff Binford thinks you should leave. Please. Listen to reason."

"Don't talk to me about reason. This is just two alpha dogs protecting the little female. Well, I'm not having it."

"You're right. That is part of it, but that's not the main part. If you're here, Amanda won't make a play for me. And if she doesn't make a play for me, she'll stay in hiding and Sheriff Binford won't be able to find her."

"I get that," Sarah said. "You're acting as bait. But what if something happens to you? What if Grady and Connor are left alone again? Have you thought of that? Are they to be bait too?"

"Nothing is going to happen to me," Tom said. "And the sheriff said if she'd wanted to get rid of the boys she would have done it when Henry was killed."

"But you can't be sure. This is all a theory you and Magnus have cooked up together. But no one knows for sure, right?"

They stood just inches apart, neither budging.

Tom sighed. "Then there is only one thing to do," he said.

Sarah raised a brow but her arms were still crossed, unbelieving.

"Get a divorce."

Sarah laughed uneasily. "Right. How can we get a divorce when we're not even married?"

He took one step and wrapped his arms around her. "I take back my proposal. We also aren't engaged."

She stiffened under his arms, but he held tight.

"You wouldn't," she said. "You're playing dirty. You would give up everything we have, everything we've gone through in the past six months. You would give it all up because you are afraid someone *might* try to hurt me?"

"Yes." He laid his chin on her head.

"I don't believe you."

"I would rather have you alive and not with me, than to have you dead and by my side. I couldn't live with myself if that happened."

She raised her head to look into his eyes. "And I couldn't live with myself if something happened to you. Do you think you are the only one who is scared of losing someone forever? What about my fears?

"How do you think Connor is going to take me leaving all of a sudden?" she continued. "We've bonded. He's lost his father, and it appears he's lost his mother as well. And if everything you suspect is true, he will lose her again when she goes to jail. He's going to need us both more than ever."

"Now you're playing dirty," Tom said.

"No, I'm telling you the truth and you know it."

Tom pulled her back down on the bed. "Let's get through this week, through Henry's funeral and then let's talk again."

"My mind isn't going to change in two days," she said.

"Maybe mine will." He stripped down to his boxers, rolled back the covers and climbed in.

Sarah came out of the bathroom wearing her usual extra long T-shirt and leggings that covered her down to the ankles and crawled in beside him. The only bits of skin showing were her feet, her hands, and her face and neck.

She spooned into him and he wrapped one arm across her waist and pulled her closer. "I can't wait until we're married and there is no longer this barrier of clothing between us."

Sarah chuckled. "What makes you think I don't sleep like this every night on my own?"

He brushed his lips along the side of her neck. "Doesn't matter. I'll enjoy taking it off piece by piece."

She sighed. "What's going to happen with us? Are we heading into a long criminal trial that will last for years? Are we staying in Broken Bow for the rest of our lives? Are we going to be immediate parents to two hurting little boys?"

"Would that be the end of the world?" He asked. "I know it's not what we planned, but maybe it is what we are meant to do—to begin again where we met and this time to make it right."

"Maybe." Sarah sighed again and closed her eyes. She concentrated on the warmth of Tom's hand across her stomach, the constant beat of his pulse against her back. At this moment, she didn't question his love. Instead, she questioned her own.

Remaining in Broken Bow meant no more scurrying up Mt. Hood to rehearse with Sweetwater Canyon. It probably meant no longer being in the band at all. She'd miss the trips with Kat and Theresa to concerts at the zoo. She'd miss the farmer's markets in the spring where the band would gauge the response of the crowd and finalize their set list for the year. She'd miss Sunday night at Pizzario's open mike where they could try out new songs with an appreciative crowd, have great pizza and beer and listen to what other local bands were doing—both beginners and touring pros.

Her eyes filled with tears of loss. She could accept leaving Portland to be with Tom, but leaving the band was something she'd never considered. Her breath caught and she curled into a tight ball, fighting off the sobs that threatened to overtake her.

"Oh, Sarah, I'm so sorry." Tom squeezed her tight. "It's all crashing in, isn't it? Come here." He levered himself slightly off the bed and turned her toward him.

She eagerly followed, turning her face into his chest. His strong arms curled around her and pulled her tight. Then he rocked her gently.

"I'm here, Sarah. I won't let you go. Let it all out. You've been holding it in a long time."

The feeling of safety in his arms and the compassion in his voice was her undoing. She let the loss overtake her in deep, soul-shaking sobs.

Her shoulders shook and her lungs struggled to catch a breath. For seven years her life had been one of keeping anything that resembled love as far away from her damaged heart as she could. She'd spent her life as a survivor of love, not a willing participant. All of her protection was falling away. The love between her and Tom and the boys overwhelmed her, exhausted her, and yet she craved it with every breath she took.

She dipped her cheek into his neck and breathed in his scent. His natural smell of earth and salt mixed with the fragrance of vanilla and coconut from the shampoo he used. She hungered for that combination of hard and soft from him. His strong, steady pulse comforted her fears.

When the sobs subsided, she slowly turned her face up to his. He kissed the tears on her cheek with soft lips. He kissed one eyelid, then the other.

"We'll work it out together," he promised. "We'll find a way for you to have everything you need."

She placed her hands on both sides of his face and pulled it closer. Her hands traced the strength of his jaw. Her eyes sought a path into his soul and her heart. Then she willingly stepped into the abyss.

She opened her heart so wide that, when Tom stepped into the maw, she imagined he placed a steel bar on either side assuring her heart could never close again. She drove her lips to his. All the words she couldn't say were forged in that kiss. Plundering, exploring, questioning she wrapped herself around him. When his tongue sought hers she captured it and sucked in his truth before releasing it and letting him explore. She no longer knew where she ended and he started. She finally felt free.

SARAH SAT in the church office for the first time since her father's funeral. She used to love going to services. She knew the pastor at this church when she was a child and, no matter what was going on at home, she'd always found solace here. But the pastor who led the church now was new. The new pastor had been called to this church a year ago. He didn't know Sarah's past, and he'd never met her father in life. He'd been kind enough, but she didn't feel she could share what was on her heart with him

Now she was here to make arrangements for Henry, and it was even harder because she didn't know much about him herself. All she knew was that he was married to Amanda and that somehow they had two amazing boys together.

Those poor boys, Sarah thought. Grady was young enough to not fully understand what had happened. He would probably recover the quickest. But Connor really worried her. He was trying so hard to be brave and helpful. But she knew how painful it was to lose a parent. Sarah had been only eight years old when her mother died. Connor was a year younger than that. Old enough to realize that death was forever, and young enough to be scared and to have nightmares about what he saw for a very long time.

When Sarah's mother died, she remembered Pastor John coming

to their home after the funeral. She'd been inconsolable when they'd lowered the coffin into the grave at the cemetery. She'd screamed for people to stop when they each took a handful of dirt and threw it on top of the coffin. She'd run away from everyone, and it took her father an hour to find her and get her home.

Once at home, Sarah had refused to come out of her room to thank all the church ladies who brought food by the house. When Pastor John came into her room to pray with her, she screamed at him. "There is no God. It's all fake. No loving God would take my mommy away."

Pastor John tried to explain that God didn't take her mother, that the cancer did. But she had countered that argument with, "If God was all powerful then why didn't he cure her mother? It was a lie. There was no heaven and no hell and no God." Finally, the pastor had resorted to saying that God needed her mommy more than she did. That her mother had an even more important job to do to help lots of other children in the world.

That had been the last straw. Sarah had yelled, "That's not true. Nothing is more important than being a mommy!" Then she burst into racking sobs. When Pastor John tried to reach down to console her, she kicked out in anger and her foot connected with his nose and broke it.

He didn't yell at her or tell her she was bad. Instead, he quietly pressed his hand against one side to try to stop the bleeding and said, "Don't go away. I'll be right back." She was sure the same God who let her mother die was going to strike her dead for hurting a pastor. In fact, she almost hoped it would happen so she could see if it was true that there was life after death.

It seemed only a minute had passed when Pastor John returned. He laid next to her on her tiny twin bed and said he was sorry to say such a stupid thing. His face was starting to bruise and swell. But he stayed there on her bed, holding an ice pack against his nose which was now also packed with gauze.

In a quiet soothing voice he said, "I know you miss your mommy, and it hurts so bad you think you're going to die. But you won't. And that hurts even more. So you just cry and scream and rage at God all you want. Get it out. It's okay. He understands. He'll wait for you."

When she'd finally run out of anger and tears, Pastor John said a prayer and asked God to watch over her and her daddy. And he told her she could come visit any time.

And she did visit. Often. And God did wait for her to come back to him.

"Miss Sarah," Pastor Larry held out his hand. "It seems I only see you for arranging funerals."

Sarah shuffled side to side a bit, feeling a little guilty for not attending even one service after her father died. "I don't really live here," she said as an excuse. "It just seems that every time I come someone dies."

"Definitely not a good sign," he said. "Perhaps we should ban you from Broken Bow."

She laughed. Maybe he wasn't so bad after all. At least he had a sense of humor.

He waved her toward a sofa. Pastor Larry's office was very different from the office she'd visited in her childhood. Instead of a large desk with the pastor sitting on one side and two chairs on the other, Pastor Larry had a round table to one side that sat in front of a large bookcase. The rest of the room held a small sofa and two occasional chairs. It felt more like a living room than on office.

After she sat, he took one of the occasional chairs across from her and crossed his leg at the knee. He held a pen and a yellow-lined tablet of paper for notes.

He leaned forward and took one of her hands in his. "I need to tell you how grateful I am that you and Tom have taken on Henry's children. Henry was a good man. He was both father and mother to Grady and Connor, and he will be sorely missed."

"You knew him then?" Sarah asked.

"Yes, he was a member of our congregation. He and the boys attended services almost every Sunday. He also volunteered with the men's group to do repair work needed around the church."

"I'm glad you know him," Sarah said. "Because I really didn't and I have no idea what he would want in a service."

"He'd want it to be light, maybe even humorous," Pastor Larry said. "He'd want his boys to be laughing instead of crying. He always told me that the boys had enough sadness in their life because of Amanda. So he believed he was called to bring light into their life whenever he could."

"Then that's what we'll do."

By the time Sarah left the pastor's office she felt as if the burdens of Broken Bow weren't as heavy. She'd shared her own story about kicking Pastor John in the nose and he'd helped her to see the humor in it. She'd talked to him about her love for Tom and the boys, and Pastor Larry had helped her to see at least two options for managing a career while maintaining a home in Broken Bow. Before she left, she mentioned that she would love to be married in this church. It was fitting that the church of her childhood—and she hoped the church of her future—would help to bridge the gaps of her life. She left with a renewed understanding of the Lord's constancy in her life.

CHAPTER 17

*T*HE BOYS LAUGHED SO HARD they couldn't stay in the pew. It was as if the entire community had come to say goodbye to Henry Davidson. And each person had heeded Pastor Larry's call for humor. They'd told stories of silliness and stories of compassion gone awry, stories of his childhood and stories of his time in the military where he was known as a man of courage, as well as a bit of a clown.

Even Tom had a story to tell. He'd helped Henry to clear out a corner of the basement to store his bottles of home brew in a cool, dry place. Connor and Grady thought it would be funny to lock them in and wait for the adults to scream in fear. But Henry saw it as a good excuse to rest instead. He and Tom swapped stories about their childhood and enjoyed some of Henry's beer. By the time the boys gave up on hoping to hear screams of fear, Henry and Tom were laughing so hard they could barely make it up the stairs and out of the basement.

This was so different from the service for Sarah's father. It made her feel good that the boys had such a wonderful role model in Henry. More than that, Broken Bow not only supported Grady and Connor, but had accepted she and Tom as a couple in that same caring community.

After the final story, Pastor Larry, took the microphone in hand

and faced the congregation. "May we all lead the life of Henry David-son. A man of faith. A man of equal strength and compassion. A man of courage. A man who loved without restraint.

"As you leave this place of worship, take Henry with you—not in tears, but in laughter. Talk of him as if he were beside you. When you hear a song or see a bird that Henry loved, know that his spirit is with you and that he continues to love you as he always has.

"Let us pray.

"May the light of God surround you, the love of God enfold you, the power of God protect you, and the presence of God dwell in you now and forever more. Amen."

Sarah lifted her face to the sunshine as they exited the church. It was a glorious day. The blue sky held only a couple of wispy clouds. The boys immediately found a group of children to play hide and seek among the trees. Long folding tables on the lawn were laden with food to be shared with all who attended. Smaller tables were strewn across the lawn with a variety of chairs beneath them so that people could sit and enjoy a meal together.

Before the service, Tom had received the church hospitality crew at the house. He'd watched them unload two cars with casseroles and vegetables and desserts to leave at home. He'd estimated they prob-ably had enough food to feed the entire family for a month.

Before she could sit down to eat, Grady ran up to Sarah and grabbed her hand. "Come help me hide, Miss Sarah. They always find me, so you have to help me hide."

Sarah laughed and ran with him to the back of the church where she remembered there was a narrow gap between two buildings where the garden tools were kept. She turned sideways to fit, then crouched behind the small plastic cabinet that held the garden equipment.

"Shhhh." She held a finger to her lips. "Don't talk so they can't find us."

Grady giggled and made himself as small as possible next to her.

She listened as the children laughed and ran from tree to tree, and searched under bushes, taunting with "I'm going to find you, Grady. You can't hide from me."

After a long period of silence she wondered if the children had given up and gone off to play something else. Just as she was ready to stand, she heard furtive steps nearby. They were slow and stopped every once in a while.

Grady peered around the shed, then tore out of Sarah's embrace. "Mommy!" he yelled.

Sarah immediately stood and came face to face with Amanda holding Grady in her arms.

"So, it's not enough that you steal Tom back from me. You've taken my children as well." Amanda's voice dripped with menace. Her eyes looked wild, like that of a trapped animal. She didn't seem to focus on any one thing for more than a moment.

Sarah looked to the end of the narrow passageway. There was no easy way out without going through Amanda and possibly harming Grady.

"Mommy, you're holding too tight." Grady squirmed in Amanda's arms.

"Stop it!" Amanda yelled. "Stop it or I'll slap you!"

Grady frowned and started to cry.

"Stop it! Stop it!" Amanda yelled again.

Grady kicked and screamed, "Put me down. I want down!"

Amanda yanked on his shirt, so that the collar constricted his breathing. "You'll do what I say or I'll show you what hurt is."

Sarah ran directly at her, tackling her and wresting Grady from her.

Amanda charged at Sarah, knocking her down onto the concrete. Sarah managed to take most of the blow so Grady wouldn't be hurt. She let Grady go and held onto Amanda's belt.

"Run, Grady," Sarah yelled. "Run and get Mr. Tom. Run fast!"

Amanda tried to chase after Grady, but Sarah held tight to the belt as she bumped along the path. Amanda made a fist and hit her in the face, but Sarah held on. Amanda continued to pummel her, yelling ugly names with each hit. Sarah tried to ward off the blows but she wasn't going to let go. She couldn't give Amanda a chance to go after Grady. She just hoped she didn't get hit hard enough to black out.

"How dare you come back for Tom after seven years! He'd forgotten you. He never loved you. Tom is mine. The farm is mine. The kids are mine. Do hear you me? Tom is mine!"

Sarah tried to stay conscious, but it was getting harder and harder. The last thing she remembered was being stuffed into the trunk of a car as Amanda said "You're dead, Sarah Cosgrave. I had to think about killing Henry, but you'll be easy. I've always hated you." Then everything went dark.

TOM COULDN'T FIND Sarah anywhere. He'd been caught up thanking everyone for coming and talking to Pastor Larry about offering a place for Sarah to stay while they pretended she'd left town.

He finally found Connor. "Have you seen your brother?" He asked.

Connor scanned the church grounds. "Uh, not lately. I think Miss Sarah was helping him play hide and seek."

"I think all the children are gone now. The game is over. I'm surprised they haven't come back."

"Mr. Tom! Mr. Tom!" Grady raced toward them from the back of the church. Tears streamed from his eyes and he had a nasty red mark across his throat.

Tom and Connor ran toward him. "What's wrong, Grady. What happened?" Tom asked.

"Mommy's mean," Grady said between gasps of breath. "Mommy hurt me. Mommy hurt Miss Sarah."

Tom wasn't sure if he was talking about something that happened long before or something new. Please, God, did Amanda show up at the funeral and he'd missed her?

"Connor, go get Pastor Larry. He's in the sanctuary. Tell him to call the sheriff and then come out here with me."

Connor turned and ran up the stairs and into the door.

Tom held Grady close. "Okay, take deep breaths. Don't try to talk yet. That's it. Take another one. Breathe in, now out. Breathe in, now out."

"Mommy took Miss Sarah away," Grady was finally able to get out. "She hurt her. Miss Sarah helped me get away and Mommy was hitting her and hitting her and there was blood everywhere just like Daddy."

Tom's pulse ratcheted faster than when he'd tried sprinting at the end of a ten mile run. If Amanda hurt Sarah he didn't know what he would do. He had to find them.

Pastor Larry and Connor joined them. "What's going on?" he asked. "Connor said Amanda's returned?"

Tom knelt on the ground in front of Grady. He took a deep breath and struggled to keep his voice calm so Grady wouldn't get even more scared. "Did you see where your mommy took Miss Sarah?"

"No. Miss Sarah told me to run and find you. I didn't look back. I had to run fast. Very fast." Grady shook as he spoke, his lips trembled and his eyes were wide with fear.

"You were very brave," Tom said. "You did the right thing. Now think carefully. Where did your mommy find you and Miss Sarah?"

"Back there." Grady pointed to the back of the church. "We were hiding by the shovels and stuff."

"The tool shed," Pastor Larry said.

"Good. You're very brave to remember that," Tom reinforced. When your mommy found you what happened?"

"I ran to her, and she picked me up, and I was happy, and she held me. But then she saw Miss Sarah and she got mad, and Miss Sarah got mad too. Then Mommy hurt me." He pointed to his throat. "She made my shirt choke me and she wouldn't stop, and Miss Sarah ran like a football player and knocked her down, and Mommy kept hitting her, and Miss Sarah told me to run and I did. I ran very fast to find you."

Tom looked at Pastor Larry. "Take the boys and call for an ambulance to come to the back lot of the church. I'm going to see if I can find anything."

Pastor Larry nodded. He took each boys hand and walked quickly back to the church reassuring Grady that he was very brave.

Tom ran full tilt to the back of the church. He scanned the treed lot, but there was no Sarah. There were no cars parked anywhere in the back. Then he searched around the tool shed for any clues, but saw nothing. He walked carefully up and down the alley between the buildings looking for something that would indicate she'd been there. But there was nothing.

Tom wasn't a praying man. He'd given up on God as a child after so many beatings from his father. But he had nowhere else to turn. *Please, God*, he prayed. *Keep Sarah alive. Help me find her.* When he saw nothing between the buildings, he slowly walked out of the alley.

Grady had said Sarah pushed Amanda down so Grady could get away. If it had happened on the concrete, there would be at least a scuff mark. He didn't see anything unusual. So, it must have been on grass or dirt. He walked slowly in a straight line, scanning to the right and the left for any clue. In the background he heard the sirens of a police car and the whoop, whoop of an ambulance. He blocked it out.

He bent to a patch of dirt and small rocks and sucked in a breath. Blood. And hair. A larger stone, maybe five inches across had the most blood on it. Had it been used a weapon? Long, golden-brown strands of hair, the same color as Sarah's, were thrown to one side. Now he could see she'd been dragged, and more long hair strands were strewn to each side. Was Amanda dragging her by the hair? He could make out a wobbly path that extended all the way to the street. As he followed the drag marks, he noticed several small bushes had leaves stripped from stems as if Sarah had tried to hold on.

The sheriff and two other officers ran toward him.

"She's gone," Tom said. "Amanda's taken her somewhere and she's hurt. That's all I know."

Sheriff Binford nodded. "We'll find her. Show me what you've found."

CHAPTER 18

Tom robotically watered the garden as the sun set on another long day. It had been a week since Amanda took Sarah. No more clues to Sarah's disappearance had surfaced, and Amanda had not contacted anyone. Tom couldn't sleep, couldn't eat. All he could think about was how he'd survive if Sarah was dead. He made hundreds of promises to God if only He kept Sarah alive. But as each day passed, he'd lost more hope. Either God didn't exist, or He chose not to listen to Tom.

The pastor took Grady and Connor back to the Rodgers farm, the temporary foster home. The sheriff agreed that if Amanda came for Tom, it wouldn't be safe for the boys. She'd already proven she was willing to hurt her own child if it meant getting what she ultimately wanted.

The Broken Bow community closed in around both the boys and Tom. The men dropped by the Davidson farm to help with chores whenever they could. No one asked questions Tom couldn't answer. The men simply provided a quiet presence and support. The women dropped by the Rodgers farm regularly. Those who had children brought them along to play with the boys. They tried to normalize Connor and Grady's day-to-day life as much as possible.

Every day Tom visited the boys and reassured them they would find Miss Sarah and their mommy. He had no good explanation for them for what had happened. When Grady asked if Mommy was mean all the time now, Tom wanted to say yes; she'd always been a mean, manipulative woman. But, even now, he couldn't bring himself to leave the boys with an image of their mother as being evil. He knew first-hand what it was like to have a bad parent. The sins of his father had been visited on Tom's soul for all his childhood and he wouldn't wish that on any child.

Tom had lived in fear of becoming like his father. It was that fear, and a feeling of unworthiness that had caused him to drive Sarah away the first time. He would not let that kind of fear brand Grady and Connor.

As darkness encroached, Tom wrapped up the hose and looked to the road that passed by the farm gate. He heard a car in the distance and watched as the headlights drew closer begging for it to stop. Instead it drove by, the headlights blinding him with light then just as quickly spitting him back into the dark.

Each day now, Tom asked only one thing of the universe. Let Amanda find him and make her demands. He would do anything she asked if it would keep Sarah alive.

His cell phone jangled in his pocket. It was an unfamiliar number. He answered.

"She'll be dead within two hours if you don't do exactly as I say."

"Amanda?" Tom breathed out the name with hope.

She laughed. "Say it again. Say my name like you love me."

Bile roiled in Tom's stomach, but he stood erect and put every effort into acting the part. He pictured Sarah in his mind. "Amanda." His voice oozed love for Sarah. "I'm sorry I've hurt you. Can we start over?"

He heard the intake of breath on the other end. Was she buying it? He tried again. "I remember the feel of your lips beneath mine, the play of our tongues. I want to feel that again."

The bile reached his throat, but he held the picture of Sarah in his mind.

"Do you want me to kill her?" Amanda asked. "Tell me to kill her then I'll believe you really love me."

Tom almost choked as he searched for something to say. "I don't want you to be blamed, my love. The sheriff already knows you killed Henry. But you can fight that. You can blame it on me. But he won't believe I made you kill Sarah."

"Because you love her!" Amanda shouted into the phone. "That's why she must die. As long as you love her, she will come between us."

"No," Tom said, a little too quickly. Then he modulated his voice. "No, I don't love her. I was using her until…until you were free from Henry. I was waiting for you, Amanda."

There was a long pause and Tom bit down hard on his tongue not to ask if Sarah was okay.

"Make me believe you," Amanda finally said.

Tom swallowed. What could he say? There was nothing about Amanda that was attractive to him. Then he knew. "Look at her," he said. "How does she even begin to compare to you?"

He heard a rustling in the distance and then a moan. "She's fat compared to me," Amanda said. "Her hair was her best feature, but I took care of that. Now she's bald like an old man." Amanda laughed hysterically. Then she shouted away from the phone. "He won't love you now that you're bald and ugly. There is nothing you have to offer."

"She told me you two still haven't screwed. Is that true?" Amanda asked.

"That's right," Tom said. "I couldn't do it because I was always thinking of you."

Amanda laughed again. "I knew it! I knew that virgin had nothing to give you. I gave it to you, Tom. I gave it to you good, didn't I?"

"You know you can always turn me on," Tom lied.

He kept repeating to himself. *Sarah is alive. She's hurt but alive. Thank you, Lord, she's alive.*

"I still have to kill her," Amanda said. "But first I want her to know how much you love me, not her. We need to do something—something together to show her. Something that will make her so sick she'll beg me to kill her."

The bile in his throat now reached his mouth. He swallowed it back down. He couldn't get sick yet. Not until he had a way to get to Sarah.

"I have an idea," he said.

"It better be good. It better hurt real good," Amanda said.

"Oh, it will, I promise. It will hurt Sarah so much you won't believe I could ever do it."

"Ooooo, tell me. If it's as good as you think, I'll tell you where I am. We can kill her together."

"That's what I was thinking," Tom said. "But before we kill her, I want to prove to you and to Sarah how much I love you."

"How?" Amanda sounded cautious.

"I want to make love to you in front of her," Tom said. "I want her to see your beautiful naked body and watch me touch you and do things with you that she would never let me do. I want her to watch me make you mine."

"Oooooo." Amanda breathed into the phone. "That's so perfect. The virgin seeing everything she missed out on and will never have. I love it! I absolutely love it!"

Tom bent over in pain as his stomach cramped.

"Then we'll kill her?" Amanda asked.

"Then we'll end this nightmare," Tom said.

Amanda gave him an address. He knew the area, it was on the far side of Broken Bow Lake where there were several abandoned cabins.

"I'll see you soon, my love."

"Wait." He heard scuffling again. "I want you to tell her you love me, not her before you hang up. I want you to tell her how we are going to make love in front of her so that she can be thinking about it for the next hour."

"Wouldn't you rather surprise her?" Tom asked. "Wouldn't the shock be better then?"

Silence.

"No. Prove to me you can tell her."

He heard more scuffling. Then a moan. "It's Tom. He has something to tell you." Amanda said, her voice not near the phone. "Here I'll hold the phone to your ear."

"Tom?"

His breath escaped and his heart skipped a beat at hearing her voice. She was alive and she could still talk.

"Sarah?"

"We're both listening," Sarah said. "What do you want to tell me?"

He understood. Sarah was smart, she knew that no matter what he said now it would not be true.

"Sarah, I'm coming over there."

"Praise the Lord. You talked Amanda in to letting me go."

He heard Amanda giggle in the background.

"No. I'm coming over there because I can finally be with Amanda, the only woman I ever really loved."

He heard her intake of breath.

"No, Tom." Sarah said, her voice sounding strangled. It actually sounded like she was crying. "No, it's not true. I love you. You can't love Amanda."

For a moment he was uncertain. Could she be this good of an actress? But he had to continue. It was the only way to save her.

"Say it again," Amanda demanded. "Say it again so she really believes you."

Tom swallowed back his doubts. "It's true," he said. "I've just been pretending with you. Every time I kissed you I was really kissing Amanda. Every time I caressed you, I was really thinking of Amanda."

"Oh God, no. Please God, don't let it be true." Sarah's sobs grew stronger.

"Tell her the rest," Amanda demanded. "Tell her what we're going to do right in front of her. Tell her!"

"I do love only Amanda," Tom said. "And I'll prove it to you. When I get there, I'm going to make sweet love to Amanda. I never touched you in that way because I was saving it all for Amanda."

"And you're going to watch," Amanda cackled. "You're going to watch every minute and see every inch of his body touching me. And I will touch him all over in a way that you will never get to touch him. You're going to watch me mark him with my mouth in every private place. Then I'll make him mine. And just when you think you can't stand it anymore, Tom and I will do it again and again until your eyes bleed from watching us."

"No. No. No." Sarah begged in the background. "Please tell me it's not true. I'll die if I have to watch you. Please, not that."

Amanda laughed hysterically. "Tell her, Tom. Tell her."

"It's all true, Sarah. That's exactly what's going to happen."

He heard heart-rending sobs in the background. His heart broke. Surely she didn't believe it would really happen that way. Or maybe even though she knew he didn't love Amanda, she was afraid he would be forced to do it anyway and she would be forced to watch. He would not let that happen. He would not hurt Sarah like that.

"That was good," Amanda purred. "That was real good. She's completely broken now. Hurry, Tom. I'm getting hot just thinking about what we're going to do together. Hurry."

The phone went dead.

Tom ran for the sink and vomited. After several minutes, there was nothing left to come up. The only thing that had kept him going was the knowledge that Sarah was alive and that he had a chance to keep her that way.

He quickly dialed the sheriff. He relayed everything that happened, and they made a plan for taking Amanda down. No sirens, no lights. In fact, no cars would show up until he was in the house at least ten minutes. His plan was to act as though everything was going to plan. If Amanda believed they were really going to have sex, she wouldn't have any weapons. She would have no way to kill when the police stormed the house.

TOM PULLED up to the cabin and stared at the candle light in the window. He sighed. Amanda was going all out for this charade. He prepared himself for seeing Sarah. He could not react with any feeling for her or Amanda might get upset. He knew she'd be bald. He suspected she'd be black and blue from the beating that happened at the church. What other horrors had she suffered?

He took a deep breath. Everything he did from now on was a matter of life and death. He had to make Amanda believe it was going to happen exactly as she planned.

He put his hat on and grabbed the bunch of roses sitting on the seat. They were blood red. He knew they were Amanda's favorite. He got out of the car and stood with his shoulders back and his spine straight like a soldier going to war. He'd taken a shower and washed the sickness out of his system. He'd also put on Amanda's favorite cologne, English Leather. He swore he'd never wear it again after Sarah left seven years ago. It reminded him what a jerk he'd been. But now it might save Sarah's life.

Somehow he put one foot in front of the other, climbed the steps to the door and knocked firmly.

Amanda opened it wearing a transparent baby doll negligee. She held a gun in one hand. With the other hand she pulled his face to her and kissed him hard, forcing his mouth to open as she thrust an angry tongue inside. He put Sarah firmly in his mind and kissed Amanda back as if she were Sarah.

When Amanda finally let go of him, he said "God I missed you. What took you so long?"

"I'm here now," Amanda said. "We will never be apart again." She took his hand and led him inside. "Come meet my guest. Sarah will be so happy to see you."

In the center of the room, a queen bed was where the dining room would have been. A chandelier, made from antlers, was turned all the way up with the lights focused on the bed. Sarah was tied to a chair facing the bed. Completely naked, her head was held in place with a cage of wires that allowed her only to look forward at the bed.

Tom's stomach lurched as he looked at her. Her bald head had been shaved with a rough razor or a knife. Several wounds oozed from her scalp. Purple and orange bruises riddled her face, and one cheekbone was significantly lower than the other, probably broken.

The welts on her chest and her arms were scabbed over as if someone hit her repeatedly with a belt or a whip. Her thighs were also cut, but not in the same way as her chest. These cuts were deeper, like those made with a knife stab.

Amanda took his hand and pulled him to Sarah. "She's disgusting isn't she? I've never seen such an ugly woman, have you?"

Tom shook his head. "I can barely stand to look at her," he said. "It's horrifying."

Amanda stared at him as if unsure what he said was good or bad. She pointed the gun at Sarah's chest. "I don't believe you."

He reached across Sarah and trailed his finger down Amanda's arm. "Such beautiful skin," he said. "Your skin is perfect compared to Sarah's."

Amanda moaned with his touch. He trailed his finger over the gun, but Amanda held her finger on the trigger.

"If you shoot her now, the blowback from the gun would get Sarah's stinky blood all over you. I'd rather make love to you first. Let me devour your beauty in the light."

Amanda withdrew the gun and minced into the light and preened. "Touch me again," she said. "Let her see how you touch me."

Tom let his fingers feather across her collar bone and then down the other shoulder. Amanda undulated under his touch.

Sarah moaned loudly.

"Yes, show her more," Amanda purred. "Let your mouth follow your fingers." She wrapped her arms around Tom's neck and arched toward him.

He audibly groaned as if he could barely hold himself back. "You're so beautiful." Then he took her hand and kissed her palm, then turned it over and kissed the back of her hand. He slowly worked his way all the way up her arm and across her shoulders. As he moved to go down the other arm toward the gun, she took his face firmly and opened her mouth.

"Kiss me in front of her. Kiss me like you did at the door. I want her to see how much you love me."

Tom again firmly put Sarah in his mind and kissed her as he did before.

Sarah cried out as if in pain, and Amanda kissed him even harder, reveling in it.

"Take off your shirt," she said.

Tom obliged and Amanda slowly ran the gun across his naked chest. She looked at Sarah. "Have you ever seen his naked chest?" She asked. "Have you ever let your mouth roam over it like this?" She trailed her tongue from his neck to where his pants stopped her.

"Stop, please stop," Sarah begged. "I can't take anymore."

Amanda laughed. "Oh you'll take more. You'll take a lot more."

"Take of your pants," Amanda instructed, "so that I can show her how a real woman pleases a man."

Tom was not going to put Sarah through that. He wondered if it was getting near the ten minutes when the sheriff would be rolling up silently outside.

He trailed his fingers across Amanda's breasts to distract her. "So round. So firm. Nothing like what I see over there." He nodded in Sarah's direction. Amanda purred beneath his touch. "I'm dying to be inside you," he said in his most seductive voice. "Let's show Sarah what love really looks like, on the bed in the full light so she can't look away."

Amanda's eyes glowed in anticipation. She moved to the bed and crawled to the middle. She laid the gun on the pillow, still within reach. She pulled up her nighty to expose everything to him.

Tom stood at the end and dropped his pants. Only his boxers covered him now.

Sarah cried openly, her sobs getting deeper.

"Dance for me," Tom said. "Strip for me. Show me every inch of your beautiful body."

Amanda smiled. She kneeled on the bed and undulated like a snake. She played with her breasts and swished her nighty back and forth, then she slowly pulled it over her head.

"So beautiful, Tom said. So amazing." He egged her on, watching for a moment when he could get the gun away from her.

She rolled onto her stomach and then got up on all fours and wiggled her bare bottom. She looked back at Tom and winked. "Show little Sarah the true animal you are. Show her how wild we can be."

Tom saw a dark figure at the window and relief poured through him. He growled like a lion and Amanda laughed.

"Close your eyes," he said, "And I'll surprise you. I'll hunt you and attack. I'll go in hard and fast."

Amanda closed her eyes. "God I'm so hot for you."

Tom growled again and then he pounced. The door crashed open. He pushed Amanda flat into the bed and pushed the gun out of reach. He put his full weight on her. Three officers surrounded the bed with guns drawn.

"Get her out of my site before I kill her myself," Tom said to the sheriff. Then he hurried to Sarah's side.

Two paramedics had cut away the wire cage and were already administering first aid to her cuts and bruises and hooking her up to an IV. A loose paper shift now covered her.

Amanda screamed in frustration as the sheriff yanked each hand behind her back and cuffed her. "You liar. You can't love her," Amanda screamed. "How could you choose her over me? She's nothing. She'll never give you what you want. She doesn't know how."

The sheriff grabbed the top sheet from the bed and covered Amanda's nakedness. Then they marched her out the door.

Tom turned to Sarah. "It's over," he said. "She'll be locked away for a long time."

Sarah nodded gingerly and smiled a crooked smile with only one side of her face.

"You have something strong going through that bag?" Tom asked pointing to the IV bag the other paramedic held.

"Morphine," he said. "In five minutes she should feel a lot less pain."

"Give us a minute," Sarah said to the paramedics.

They nodded and stepped away to prepare the gurney.

"I'm sorry I had to play along with Amanda. You knew it was all pretend to save you, right?"

"I never doubted you for a minute. You knew all my sobbing was pretend, right?"

He shook his head. "I hoped, but I wasn't sure."

Tom bent toward her, a hand on either side of the chair. "Does anything not hurt?" he asked.

"My left eyebrow."

He feathered a kiss there.

"Anywhere else?"

"My lower lip. She didn't get that."

He rained a series of kisses from one side of her lip to the other.

"Have they checked out your neck? Your back?"

"It's okay," she said. Nothing broken, except maybe a couple ribs. Mostly lots of bruising from all the punches I took at the church."

"And the cuts?" Tom asked. "A knife?"

"Mostly a belt with a sharp buckle. She really hated me, and using the belt on me each day made her feel a little better. After you made the date, she took a knife to my thighs. She said something about you'd never see my thighs without scars."

Tom raked a hand through his hair. "I'm so sorry."

"It's not your fault. Amanda is a nut job."

"But if I'd never—"

She held a finger to his lips to silence him. "Let's not give her any more thoughts today. In fact, I'd rather not even hear her name until I answer more questions for the police."

Tom made a little X over his chest. "Cross my heart. No mention of she who will not be named."

Sarah stared at Tom's chest. "I *have* seen your naked chest before. And your boxers." She sighed. "But they crashed the door in before I could see what was underneath."

He shook his head. "You're amazing. After all you've been through, that's what you're thinking?"

"I had to distract myself from the pain," she said.

"How can I make it up to you?" Tom asked.

"I'm thinking we better get married real soon, so I can see what's in those boxers."

"I could drop them right now and show you if that would make you happy."

She barely lifted her lips this time to smile. "I've waited this long," she said. "What's another few days."

"Then let's get you to the hospital as quick as possible. The minute the doctor gives you the all clear, I'll be at the altar waiting." Tom turned to the paramedics and motioned them over.

"Ready to go to the hospital, Miss Cosgrave?" the taller paramedic asked as he moved to one side of her chair.

The second man stood on either side. "How is your pain level?"

"A lot better, I think," Sarah said. "I'm getting a little sleepy."

"That's good. Now, we're gonna lift you real slow and easy unto the gurney. It might hurt a bit."

"I'd prefer that Tom carry me to the ambulance," she said. "I've waited too long to have his arms around me again."

"That's not exactly protocol, ma'am."

"Will I hurt her if I carry her?" Tom asked.

"It would be better to get her flat on the gurney first," the paramedic holding the IV bag said. "Then we can stabilize her before lifting her into the ambulance."

"Let's compromise," Tom suggested. "I'll lift her onto the gurney, and then you can take her to the ambulance."

"And you'll ride with me to the hospital," Sarah said.

"Of course. I wouldn't be anywhere else."

Tom gently placed one arm under her knees, and then worked his other arm behind her back. "Ready?"

She nodded.

"Deep breath."

"Can't," she said. "The ribs."

"I love you, Sarah Cosgrave." He lifted her and she hardly even whimpered. "I've got you," he said.

She laid her head against his shoulder.

"And I love you, Tom Pawlak. Till death do us part."

EPILOGUE

NE YEAR LATER

SARAH WOKE and rolled over to look at her husband. Marriage was so much better than she ever imagined. She never knew how close two people could be, how they could anticipate each other's needs both in bed and in life.

She also never knew what a joy a small, close-knit community could be. She still missed Portland and the chance to rehearse with Sweetwater Canyon but, in spite of her years in Portland, she'd never managed to find close friends outside of the band. Broken Bow, on the other hand, was like a big, raucous family. She had her church family, and a family of mothers with children, and she'd found a musical family too with some local bluegrass musicians who loved having her join sessions whenever she wanted.

Connor pulled a sleepy Grady into the room and they both climbed onto the end of the bed. He pushed on Tom's back. "Daddy, it's time to get up," he said. "We have to get ready and leave. The plane is leaving soon for Portland. And we get to tour with the band"

"And ride in Annabelle," Grady added.

Tom rolled over and pulled Sarah into his embrace. "We have plenty of time," he said. "The plane doesn't leave for six hours and we are all packed."

"Six whole hours?" Connor whined. "That's forever."

"Not even close to forever," Tom said. "Go fix some toast for you and Grady. Mommy and I want to sleep some more. We were up late packing." His eyes twinkled as he looked at Sarah and she blushed.

"You always want more time," Connor said, drawing out the word 'always.'

"That's right," Tom said. "We always want more time. Love wants more time."

Connor reluctantly crawled off the bed and took Grady by the hand. "Come on. They want to make boring kissy faces. Let's go have breakfast."

Sarah giggled. Kissy faces were so fun.

"Are you excited about touring again with Sweetwater Canyon," Tom asked.

She nodded. "I'm even more excited that you and the boys are coming with us. I never thought I could live here and still be part of the band. They were so sweet to still keep a space for me, even if it's only for summer."

"They love you," he said.

"Yes, they do." She snuggled into his embrace. "But not as much you."

He chuckled. "At least not in the same way."

"And we all have children in school now too," she said. "Both Rachel and Michele don't want to tour as much anymore either. And Kat's off to college in the fall. So, the timing was perfect for me to leave Portland."

Sarah ran a finger through the hair on Tom's chest. "It will be fun to see how Connor and Grady fit in with the other kids. I'd love for them all to learn instruments and join us on stage once in a while, like Claire does with Rachel on the fiddle."

"Let's not get ahead of ourselves, now. Connor and Grady may have other ideas, more like wanting to be on the management end of things with me."

"Already want to pass along the family business?" Sarah asked.

Tom smoothly rolled her underneath him, and slowly worked kisses from her forehead to her eyelids, and then to each cheek. When he moved to her lips, his kisses were softly entreating. She couldn't help but answer his call.

"Do you want any more kids, or are two enough?" he asked, as his passion grew.

"More," she said. "Do you?"

"At least two more. I like even numbers. Maybe a couple girls would be nice."

She smiled. "Girls or boys are fine with me."

"If we start now, maybe we could have enough for a Sweetwater Canyon softball team," he said.

She grinned. "Then let's try for twins."

KEEP IN CONTACT

JOIN MY MAILING LIST

Want to keep up with new books about the women of Sweetwater Canyon? Then be sure to join my mailing list. It's on the front page of my website. http://maggielynch.com Get access to free short stories, giveaways only for those on the mailing list and special discounts on future books.

CONSIDER WRITING A REVIEW

Word-of-mouth is crucial for any author to succeed. If you enjoyed the book, please consider leaving a review on Amazon, Barnes and Noble, Kobo, GoodReads, Library Thing, Shelfari, or anywhere else you tend to look for new books. Even if it is only a line or two, it would make all the difference and would be very much appreciated

ABOUT THE AUTHOR

Maggie Lynch is the author of 20+ published books, as well as numerous short stories and non-fiction articles. Her fiction tells stories of men and women making heroic choices one messy moment at a time. Her nonfiction focuses on helping indie authors be successful in their careers. Maggie is also the founder of Windtree Press, an independent publishing cooperative with over 200 titles among 20 authors.

Maggie and her musician husband live in the beautiful Pacific Northwest, and are the slaves of two demanding cats. In 2013, after careers in counseling, the software industry, academia, and worldwide educational consulting, Maggie chose to devote her time to her career as a full time author.

https://maggielynch.com
maggie@maggielynch.com